While the Black Stars Burn

Published by Raw Dog Screaming Press
Bowie, MD

First Edition

Cover: Daniele Serra
Book design: Jennifer Barnes
Printed in the United States of America
ISBN: 978-1-935738-77-0
Library of Congress Control Number: 2015955041

www.RawDogScreaming.com

While the Black Stars Burn

Lucy A. Snyder

Contents

Mostly Monsters

My bones dragging like lead rods, I trail after my girlfriend on her quest for yarn in some huge, fluorescent craft barn. The lights are buzzing brain bleach. I spy with my bloodshot eye modeling clays in kid-friendly buckets, bright packs of rainbow logs. I want them desperately. I want to grab a pack and run off to some dark, quiet room and feel the cool, greasy clay squish and roll beneath my fingers. But even the cheapest, tiniest pack is $10 and my car needs gas and my husband's surgery is coming up and there's no room in our little house to build anything. I pass on by.

In my girlfriend's car, I close my eyes in the summer heat and remember the smell of the clay as I worked at my craft on a card table in the back bedroom of my father's house. The walls seemed to hold their breath before the air conditioner thumped on. In that dusty, silent room of a ranch house surrounded by ancient neighbors who weren't anyone's grandparents, I used to build my friends: dragons and squires and heroines, but mostly monsters.

My mother started me on monster making. When I was little I had vivid dreams, sometimes terrifying ones, and I told her about the scary creatures who came to me at night.

"When you see them, just make friends with them," she said cheerfully. "Then you'll see they're not so bad."

My mother was a lucid dreamer, and when I was older I realized she was encouraging me to take control of my nightmares. But I was never any good at that, not even as an adult, and when I was five I didn't understand. How would I know when I'd see them again? How could I possibly wait for that? So I recreated the monsters in clay to make them fight each other and not chase me through the woods or through strange houses with endless corridors.

I made my own Godzilla in gray and green clay and a muscular Wolf Man in brown. There was blue, eight-armed Tentacles (pronounced like Hercules), whom I started dreaming about after I glimpsed the giant squid scene in *20,000 Leagues Under the Sea* on TV. And there was Eyeblob, a formless mass of eyeballs that had chased me 'round and 'round in my dreams ever since I could remember. Playing with my creations didn't stop the rare nightmares, but it didn't make them worse, either, and after all there wasn't anybody else to play with.

One evening, my parents forgot why they'd told me to keep the clay in the back room and they let me bring my creations out to play on the coffee table while they watched television. My friends menaced one another in the flickering blue light. Afterward, it was time for bed. I put my monsters away and soon I was soundly out in the kind of sleep only a kid can have.

Suddenly my father burst into my bedroom, shouting about the coffee table. The clay left smudges on the glass! He dragged me into the living room. Disoriented, terrified, I was sobbing, pleading. He threw a napkin at me and made me scrub at the stubborn smudges with a shivering hand. I couldn't keep the snot and tears from dripping off my nose onto the table and that made him angrier, louder. My mom hovered nearby, quietly asking him to stop. Not intervening. She didn't tuck me in afterward. For a long time, I thought she'd done all she could to stop him.

Thirty-seven years later, I tell a perfect stranger in a therapy room that, if it had been me, I wouldn't have just stood by making helpless mouth noises while my bad marital choice did that to my kid. The moment he headed to the bedroom, I'd have told the fucker that the Windex was under the sink if the smudges were such a catastrophe. And if he'd opened that door and said anything more than "I love you" he would have spent the night outside with the bats.

The perfect stranger asks me how my relationship with my father is. We aren't friends. He asks how my sleep is. It's shit.

Every night I wake up in a panic, thinking I have forgotten something critical and now a man is coming into my room to punish me. Kill me. *Every. Fucking. Night.* Sometimes six or seven times a night. And when I'm awake, I feel as though I'm always holding my breath, waiting for the thump.

The perfect stranger tells me I have PTSD. He says that pills—which I never asked for anyhow because I hate how they smear my brain—won't help. I need complex, long-term therapies to repair my broken sleep, and my insurance mostly won't cover it. The bills would be a devouring beast.

My girlfriend drives me home. I roll the letters around in my head. PTSD. From that? One harsh wakeup in a silent house? *Seriously*?

But it wasn't just that. The kind of guy who would roust his kid screaming over a few clay smudges wouldn't do only that. His violence was rare, but memorable, the work of some great anti-artist slowly building me up only to tear me back down. I marvel again that my mother stayed with him the decade it took for me to be conceived, and I also want to weep because she stuck with him 'til her death, thirty-five years more.

Girlfriend drops me at the curb and I go inside, quiet so I don't wake my husband from his nap upstairs. Our coffee table is scarred wood, piled with prescriptions and junk. I climb the stairs, take off my clothes and slip into the sheets, my body spooning against my husband's perfectly. He shifts, murmurs, starts to snore again. I don't sleep. I think of the deplorable clutter on the coffee table, and our bills, and wish I'd bought a bucket of clay anyhow.

Finally I get up and go to my computer in our back bedroom. There are smudges on the monitor screen. I don't wipe them off. I take a deep breath, and start to write about dragons and squires and heroines, but mostly monsters.

Spinwebs

Adira held the cabbage-sized, iridescent amber egg close to her chest while Mama Silklegs twitched and curled on the hay-stuffed mattress. The gentle old spinweb was wheezing in obvious agony, the lids over her four eyes swollen. Mama curled her eight legs under her in a strange way; the tears blurring Adira's eyes made the old spinweb look like a massive copper daisy sagging on her parents' bed. A sour odor like spoiled chicken broth hung in the air.

Solemn, her father dripped milky poppy tonic from a goatskin into Mama's round, toothy mouth. He'd given Adira's grandmama the same tonic when her belly swelled as if she were with child but no child ever came. Her grandmama said the tonic took away the pain in her bones and helped her sleep. Adira hoped it would help Mama, too.

She wanted so badly to be strong like her parents told her, but Adira couldn't stop the tears burning in her eyes. Even replaying within her mind the ridiculous songs her Aunt Ruthie taught her didn't help. Her brother Moshe and sister Dalia were weeping openly, clutching their eggs like they used to hold tight to their baby blankets during thunderstorms.

"Don't squeeze them so! Just keep them warm!" Gray-faced, her mother wiped her own eyes on her apron. Her own health failed when Mama got sick; their father said it was from worry but Adira knew it was more than that. Just a year ago her mother had been a big, hearty woman who could heft 60-pound rolls of silk damask over her head into the merchant's wagon. While her will remained strong, her body was frighteningly thin. Adira feared that a strong winter wind might blow their mother away.

She put a shaky hand on Adira's shoulder. "It is the way of things. Having babies is hard on her, just like it is for us."

The girl silently vowed to never have a baby. "I don't want her to die."

"None of us do, my little mouse. She is a queen amongst the spinwebs; she has lived a long and wonderful life and provided for five generations of our family. There will be none like her again, but she has left us three beautiful eggs, and she trusts us to raise her babies. None could hope for so great an honor as this."

Moshe sniffled. "Not even Prince Helmut?"

Mother snorted. "Certainly not he."

Their father emitted a strangled noise somewhere between a nervous laugh and a muffled yelp. "Darling! Do not tell the children such things; they might repeat them outside, and then what would happen?"

Muscles bunched at her mother's gaunt jaw. "I forgot myself. Children, as your father says: say nothing of Prince Helmut's greed and villainy."

"Darling!"

"I take it back," she sighed. "Children: forget!"

Mama Silklegs emitted a sudden pained shriek and thrashed on the bed, and in almost the same moment their mother clutched at her chest and fell to her knees, her face contorted in pain.

Adira sat watch over her mother while her father and the weavers and dyers dug a grave for Mama in the family graveyard. The girl's stomach ached with fear. Her mother fainted when Mama died, and none could wake her. Mama had to be buried before sunset, and digging such a massive grave took almost all the able-bodied people on the magnanery. So her father put her mother in Adira's bed and told the girl to fetch him if her condition worsened.

She hugged the egg in her lap. The iridescent shell was hard like oil-boiled leather, but she could feel the baby spinweb moving inside, stretching the walls. It would hatch soon. She knew she had to take the best possible care of the egg, not just out of respect for Mama but also because the only spinweb who remained, Auntie Goldbelly, produced barely a quarter of what Mama had before her egg sickness. They grew plenty of vegetables and raised goats, but if they didn't sell enough silk, they wouldn't be able to pay Prince Helmut's new tax. The dairy farmer next door hadn't been able to pay after his cows poisoned themselves on ragwort, and soon the prince's guard came with crossbows and swords and seized the farm. Adira's father sheltered the evicted farmer and his family for a few months, but they left to seek a better fortune in Esterland, whose queen was said to treat her subjects fairly.

"How is she?" Her father stood in the doorway, drying his hands on a dishcloth. Graveyard mud stained the knees of his grey silk trousers.

"Much the same," Adira replied, feeling an ache in her chest. "I tried singing her favorite song, but it didn't help."

Her father moved to the head of the bed and gently lifted her mother's eyelids and peered down at her constricted pupils. With a sad shake of his head, he stood up, tugging on his long black beard as he always did when he was upset.

"Is it bad?" Adira asked, feeling herself tear up again.

"It is," he replied. "Losing Mama was a terrible shock to her soul. When Mama hatched, she first bonded to your great-grandmother, who was a girl no older than you. Spinwebs live so long that they are accustomed to losing their people, but for your mother to lose her Mama? It's a dire thing. Your mother surely felt it as keenly as if she herself had died."

He cleared his throat. "I can make an elixir that might revive her, but I need a quantity of tutsan, and the hills are barren of flowers."

The girl sat up straighter, thinking. There was a plan. She could *do something* instead of just sitting helplessly. "Won't the apothecary have powdered herbs?"

Her father paused. "Fresh would be best, but I *could* use dried petals...."

"Dalia could stay with mother, and I could go fetch them for you?" Adira loved the apothecary shop with its colorful glass bottles and exotic smells and mysterious compounds. She immediately felt a little guilty for wanting to be there instead of at her mother's side. But not guilty enough to take back her suggestion. "It's not far. I wouldn't be gone long."

"All right." Her father sounded reluctant. "I suppose it *is* only a mile away. But take Moshe with you. And a knife. And mind the eggs! Do not let anything happen to them. I have harnesses for both of you...."

Their father went through his chests and found egg harnesses made from thick sheepskins, leather straps and shiny brass buckles. He helped them put on the harnesses and strap the eggs inside the cozy sheepskin cradles. He gave Adira one of his hunting knives, and she secured the sheath to her belt.

Moshe giggled when she buttoned her long blue padded silk coat over the harness. "You look like you ate a barn!"

"So do you!" she replied, which did nothing to stifle his laughter.

"Children, be serious." Their father drew them in close. "Your mother would skin me if she knew I was letting you go out with the eggs. I should send one of the weavers or dyers, but the truth is that I cannot spare them from their work. I am terribly afraid that we won't get a good price for our cloth, so we need to make twice as much to ensure that we have the tax money when the soldiers come next month."

He paused, and Adira knew his unspoken fear: that if they waited to get the ingredients for the elixir, her mother would not recover.

"We will be fine." She squared her shoulders, determined to stay as brave as she could. "We've been there a hundred times! And there are so many soldiers on the road that nobody has seen a bandit in months."

Her father frowned at the floor when she mentioned soldiers. "I suppose that's one silver lining."

Then he looked at Adira: "Are you ready?"

She stuck her hand in her right coat pocket, turned it out, and ripped a hole in the seam so she could draw the knife if she needed to. "I'm ready."

Just inside the city wall, Adira and Moshe encountered a group of older boys in black students' robes clogging the road, laughing and shoving one another. Her heart beat faster; big boys were trouble. She tried to lead Moshe around the gang, but one, the tallest boy, noticed them and threw out a gangly arm to block their way.

"Ugh," he said, wrinkling his nose at them in exaggerated disgust. His blond hair fell in fashionable ringlets around his face. She could tell from the cut of his tunic beneath his robe that his parents were wealthy burghers.

"You stink of spiders," he said, stepping aggressively close.

Adira squeezed Moshe's hand and gave him a quick, meaningful glance. *Say nothing.*

Moshe gave her a quick nod in reply and stared down at his boots.

Another boy stepped up. He had close-cut brown hair and the wispy beginnings of a beard. "Spiders are an *abomination.* We shouldn't allow people who live with *abominations.*" He pronounced it as though it was the first really long word he had learned in school and he'd been dying to try it out.

Adira tried to swallow her anxiety and aggravation. She wanted to tell him that comparing her family's spinwebs to common house spiders was like comparing humans to field mice, but she knew he'd never understand.

"Spinwebs made your robes and your mothers' fancy dresses," she replied. "Maybe you should all go naked if you think they're so bad."

The second boy blushed and stepped back, but the first boy scowled down at her.

"My father dines with the prince, and he says foul daggles like you have no place in our kingdom. Your days here are *few,*" he whispered.

"I'm sure that's true." Her nerves sang with fear and anger. The feeling made her a little sick, but it felt good, too, like she was finally really alive. Her own emotions scared her even more than the boys did, so she tried to push all the fear away. She slipped her hand into her pocket, feeling the smooth knob of the knife's pommel, wondering if the bully was the sort of soft boy who would panic at the sight of his own blood, or if he would fly into a murderous rage. Either way, the guards would surely come. And then what? Her mind flew over a hundred different scenarios, and they all seemed bad or catastrophic. The guard and townsfolk would rally behind the boys, not her and Moshe.

Her spinweb kicked inside its shell, reminding her of her duty. No. She couldn't resort to the knife, not here.

She forced a meek, unassuming smile. "But since our days are numbered, can we please go about our business? Surely the prince will expunge us and you will never have to see us again."

"But I have to smell your stink *now.*" He eyed her as if she was a bit of cow dung that refused to be scrubbed from his shoe. "Ugh, I can't see how you live with it! Is it coming from your clothes? What have you got there under your coats?"

Adira gave Moshe's hand another squeeze, and neither of them spoke.

"What have you got?" the blond boy demanded. "You better tell me, or I'll call for the guard!"

She couldn't think of a good lie, so she told the truth: "Spinweb eggs."

He frowned. "What?"

"Eggs. Our mama spinweb is having babies, and we're keeping them warm for her," she said.

"Nasty," the second boy hissed, and he and the others backed away a bit, staring at the egg bulges as though they might suddenly hatch and swarm the boys.

The blond boy didn't budge. "Maybe we should take those eggs and smash them."

Everyone fell silent. Her heart was pounding so loudly she was sure the boys could hear it. Her spinweb trembled against her belly as though it had understood the threat.

Adira's thoughts raced. What could she say now? This bully was either a predator or fancied himself as one. She remembered what her father told her about wolves: *Don't run, or they'll think you're prey. Don't show fear.*

"Well." Adira spoke slowly, trying to seem calm, trying to still her heart and steady her voice. "You *could* do that. But if you think we stink now? Imagine what the inside of a broken egg smells like. Even *we* can't stand it."

She gazed up into the blond boy's eyes and let her smile go mad. "If you break the eggs, the stink will be on you *forever*. And Mama Silklegs will know you killed her babies. She will sniff you out and find you in your bed at night when you're asleep. She'll inject you with a poison to paralyze you, but you'll still feel everything. She'll cut a hole in your belly and pull your intestines out and eat them like noodles while you're still alive. And you'll want to scream and scream, but you won't be able to. She'll take her time, and it will take you hours to die. But when she's done, you'll be good and dead and your own mother won't recognize what's left of you."

Everyone stared at her, horrified.

"You're lying," the boy stammered.

"You sure?" She smiled wider.

Blanching, the boy stepped back and joined his comrades, clearing the cobblestone path to the apothecary's. Adira pulled Moshe forward and they marched on.

"That was a good lie," Moshe whispered when they were out of earshot.

"What makes you think I was lying?" she whispered back, feeling elated that her bluff had worked.

"But Mama Silklegs is dead!"

She stared down at him. "Do you think death would stop her from avenging her children's murder?"

Her baby spinweb kicked inside its shell.

Moshe shivered. "But Mama was kind and gentle. She'd never hurt anyone like you said she would."

"Maybe not like that," Adira admitted. "She *was* kind and gentle. With *us*. But do you remember the bandits who kicked in the door and tried to carry mother away?"

Moshe nodded uncertainly. "Mama chased them off?"

She shook her head. "She ate them. Swallowed them down like goats. We told you they ran so you wouldn't have bad dreams."

When they got home from the apothecary, Adira gave her father the tin of powdered flowers.

"Did you and Moshe mind your eggs?" he asked.

"Of course." She unbuttoned her coat to show him.

His eyes widened. "What has happened to it?"

She looked down. The egg had turned a deep scarlet, red as roses and blood.

"I—I don't know," she replied. "It didn't get so much as a bump."

"Did it get too hot, maybe?" Her father put his ear to the top of the shell and listened for several minutes.

"The baby is moving fine," he finally said. "I have never seen an egg turn this color, but I certainly have not seen everything in the world. Take care of it, and I'll take care of your mother, and we'll both hope for the best."

It took her father most of the evening to brew the elixir. Adira had high hopes when he brought it into the sickroom, but even after he got a whole teaspoon down her mother's throat, nothing happened.

"Well." Disappointment was plain on his face. "Don't lose hope, child. Sometimes it can take the elixir a while to work. I'll give it to her every few hours; in the meantime, keep watch and let me know if her breathing changes."

Adira spent most of the next three days in her mother's sickroom, alternately singing songs to her mother and silently petting the scarlet egg, hoping both of them would be all right.

On the fourth day, the egg nearly jerked out of her hands when the baby gave a very strong kick. And the shell had cracked!

"Father! Father, come quick, I think it's hatching!"

Her father and Moshe and Dalia rushed into the room.

"Mine's not hatching; when does mine hatch?" Moshe complained.

The baby spinweb kicked again, and a hairy crimson leg poked through a fracture in the shell.

"Help it come out," her father encouraged. "Carefully!"

Adira began to pull bits of loose shell and tough membrane away, and the baby spinweb kicked mightily with all eight legs until the hole was big enough to struggle through. The newly-hatched spinweb was damp, but his fur was soft as dandelion fluff and so very bright, a much braver red than any dye she had seen. His four eyes were the brilliant blue of a cloudless winter sky.

From the corner of her eye, Adira saw her mother stir on the bed.

"Guardian..." her mother whispered. Her crackling voice was filled with awe.

"My lord!" her father breathed. "He *is* a guardian! Our family has not seen one in over a century."

"A guardian?" Adira wondered aloud. "Will he make a different kind of web?"

The baby touched her face with one long leg, and she met his gaze. A strange warm buzzing filled her mind, and for a moment she was dizzy.

No webs. I only...protect. You protect. We save family.

Just as Adira realized she was hearing the hatchling's voice inside her own head, a quick succession of prophetic images flashed through her own mind, images of the royal guards kicking in the door just as the bandits had, of her unarmed father falling beneath vicious sword blows, her mother weeping over Moshe's bloodied corpse. And most of all, fire, fire everywhere, and the spinwebs wailing as flaming roof beams rained down upon them.

The prince will bring terror, the guardian said, his voice stronger and clearer in her mind.

"Why? Why would he do that?" The images he'd put in her mind were so terrible she wanted to vomit.

Hatred. It has hatched in the town. They need someone to blame for the troubles the prince is causing, and he has chosen us. I saw the boys' minds, saw the foulness their parents and priests are teaching them, and I knew I had to alter myself. You and I can stop the future I have glimpsed.

"How?" It was hard to talk, hard to breathe. "How can we stop it?"

Distantly, she heard her little brother ask, "Why's she saying that?" only to be shushed by their father.

You can change, too. There is time before the prince's mind-poison spreads so much that the townsfolk abandon their own religion's teachings and turn to violence against us. We will both become warriors for our peoples before that happens. If you are willing.

In her mind, she saw herself traveling to a kingdom in the south where strong men and women rode proudly atop mighty armored spinwebs. She saw herself training her body and mind, learning to fight with her hands and a sword and a lance atop her scarlet spinweb. But most of all, she saw herself sitting with an old priestess, learning to use words and her wit to douse the fire of an angry opponent's violence. It was a vision she liked better than any of her own daydreams.

Not spinwebs, he corrected. *We spin no webs. We hunt those who are violent, and we protect those who are peaceful. We are* Akavishim.

"Akavishim," she repeated, and she heard her parents gasp.

What do I call you? she asked.

Brother Firebelly, he replied. *I am yours.*

"And I am yours."

The Strange Architecture of the Heart

Mira watched her husband Jeffrey draw invisible signs in the air in front of the couch. He'd been planted there for hours; she couldn't tell if he was coding or gold farming. His blue sensory visor was tight across his eyes and ears. She couldn't hear the music, or whatever he was listening to, but clearly it was loud enough to drown out the thunderous crack of the bomb exploding down the street.

She hesitated, then stepped forward and tapped him gently on his left shoulder. His whole body jerked in surprise, and he hit the button on the side of his visor to turn the digital lenses transparent.

"What's up?" He gazed up at her through his smudged glasses, looking annoyed and disoriented.

"Another one got through the shields. Down the street. It took out the United Dairy Farmers store." The Hand of God southern apocalyptic cult had been blown to microscopic ash in a government anti-terrorism raid, but their cloaked Khishchnik satellite was still in high orbit somewhere, periodically sending honeybee-sized fusion bomb drones down to random northern cities. It was the most senseless of senseless violence, but nobody in charge seemed able to stop it. Or they didn't have the political will to stop it. Either way, experts guessed that the satellite was packing more than ten thousand drones.

"Oh, jeez." He blinked, his eyes focusing on her a bit more. "Anybody hurt?"

"Four killed, they're saying. A woman and her two little boys. And the store clerk." Mira felt sick picturing them all lying there in pieces in the rubble. She hoped they hadn't suffered. The boys' father had to be beside himself with grief. She didn't know him or his dead family, but she could imagine what he was going through.

"Damn." An expression of sympathy attempted to crawl across her husband's face, but it died past his lips. "Well, when it comes, it comes."

He lifted his hand to tap the button and shut her out again, but she reached out and put her hand on his. Her heart quickened in her chest; she was too nervous to say *I miss you. Please make love to me*, so instead she stammered, "I'm scared. Could you come upstairs with me for a while?"

It wasn't a lie. The drones scared the shit out of her. They killed her father. They killed her girlfriend Amy. There wasn't a damn thing she could do to protect herself or anyone else, except move down south. Which meant leaving everyone they knew and everything they'd worked for and becoming refugees. All the Southern cities were bursting with people and housing was so expensive that they'd be broke in a matter of months even if she found decent work on top of Jeffrey's job. It felt like they'd be trading the possibility of a quick death with the certainty of slow starvation.

"Please?" she said.

Jeffrey opened his mouth to say something, then closed it, going silent for two or three seconds. In those fleeting moment she imagined that they went upstairs, hand-in-hand, and he lay down with her to cuddle, and soon they were kissing, and then they were having sex for the first time in five years.

And then she imagined that she got pregnant, and she didn't miscarry like last time. She imagined she gave birth to a healthy baby who had his blue eyes and her curly brown hair, and she imagined she finally had a family. She imagined what it would be like to feel the weight of her baby's warm head in the palm of her hand. She imagined what it would be like to have a toddler grab her legs and say "I wuv you, Mama!" She imagined no longer having to sneak off and cry in the women's restroom when the young secretaries announced their pregnancies at her office.

"I really need to work," he said. The same thing he'd said every night since she miscarried. He'd seemingly convinced himself that if he just stayed busy enough, he'd never have to face his own grief over losing their child.

She felt all her fragile imaginings crumple into nothing.

"*Please*?" she whispered.

"There's a 30% bonus if I can get this deployed by midnight." He looked puzzled, then frowned in concern toward the kitchen. "Is Rachel malfunctioning?"

Heat rose in her face. "No. I just...wanted to be with you...."

His expression was blank, distant. "I'm really busy. Sorry."

The sudden spike of anger felt like battery acid in her chest. But she made herself smile. "Fine."

She turned away and went into the kitchen, where Rachel was kneading bread and humming Christmas carols. Just ever-so-slightly off key, sometimes; it was part of her naturalistic programming.

Rachel was a Juno 2500 Personal Assistant Android. She'd been Amy's, purchased via the proceeds of a large National Science Foundation grant awarded to Amy's lab. Rachel started as a gene sequencing slave, but soon she was upgraded to work as Amy's personal assistant at conferences and was quite well-received at poster sessions.

Amy brought Rachel with her when she visited three years before. Jeffrey didn't care that his wife had a girlfriend; he probably wouldn't have cared if she had a boyfriend, either, but at the time that felt like a step too far to Mira. Mira took Amy upstairs and they made love while Rachel made them all dinner. Afterward, Amy decided to go to the store to find a kind of Riesling she liked.

A honeybee drone hit her on the way home; there wasn't anything left of her to bury.

Mira spent weeks lost in a fog of depression; when she emerged, she realized that Rachel was still puttering around their townhome. Apparently, nobody from Amy's university had come looking for Rachel or had even asked about her; everyone assumed she had been vaporized along with her mistress.

Furthermore, Jeffrey had changed Rachel's serial number records in the national database and had programmed her with additional behaviors and skill sets. Mira discovered this when, after one of her crying jags, Rachel gently hugged her and oh-so-politely asked if cunnilingus might take her mind off things.

As it turned out, it did.

Since then, Mira had used a big chunk of the money she'd been saving for adoption search fees to swap out Rachel's decorative genitalia with a fully functional package modeled on that of a male porn star whose movies Mira intended to never see.

"Rachel," Mira said.

The lovely android stopped kneading the dough and turned, smiling expectantly. A millisecond later her face took on a perfect expression of concern. "You look so sad! What's the matter?"

"I'd like you to take me upstairs and fuck me unconscious."

"Okay, but…I think your blood sugar is low. You should eat something. I can make you a snack?" Rachel wiped her hands off on her apron.

The android was equipped with a multitude of bioscanners and was never wrong about such things. "Okay. Fix me whatever."

Rachel carefully set the dough aside in a glass pan, draped it with a damp tea towel, and made a perfect, tiny peanut butter sandwich and poured her a half-glass of milk to go with it. Mira dutifully ate it.

"Do you feel better?" Rachel asked.

"I do, thank you. Now, please take me upstairs…."

Afterward, Mira fell into a hard sleep on Rachel's soft, lifelike bosom. Unlike Jeffrey, Rachel would not have a bad dream at 3am, slip out of bed and go work on the couch. Unlike Jeffrey, Rachel would not start perspiring in the middle of the night and fill Mira's ears with trickling sweat. Unlike Jeffrey, Rachel could never get her pregnant.

Mira woke and quietly began to weep.

Rachel stirred. "There, there. What's the matter?"

"I want a baby," Mira confessed. She felt like a loser saying it out loud. Here she was, nearly forty, a damnable cliché of a woman with a ticking biological clock. And she was in no position to have a child, not physically, not logistically, not in any way. It took a village to raise a child, she knew, and had no village. She didn't even know their neighbors' names. Worst of all, she couldn't talk herself out of her heart's desire. "I want a baby so badly and I can't have one. Jeff won't help me…."

"I would be glad to help you care for a child," Rachel said.

"I'd need Jeff to fuck me at least once," Mira replied bitterly.

"You could get artificial insemination." Rachel sounded slappably cheerful. "Or you could adopt."

"All of which require money. Which I…have spent on other things." Her shoulders sagged at the admission. *The one thing I want most in the world, and I just don't want it badly enough to actually do anything about it. Loser.*

"Like what?" Rachel chirped.

"Like you. Your upgrades, anyhow."

"Oh." The lovely android paused. "What about a boyfriend?"

"What about one?"

"A boyfriend could get you pregnant at low or no cost!"

"Rachel, baby, if I could get myself a boyfriend, I'd be with him this very minute."

The next night, Rachel went out to go grocery shopping and was gone for so long that Mira began to fear that she'd been stolen. The tracking software on her phone said the android was about four blocks away from where she should be. In a nightclub, of all places. Had she been kidnapped? Mira didn't know if she should call the police or just keep waiting. She paced while Jeffrey did his technological pantomimes on the couch, oblivious.

But then Rachel came through the front door, half-carrying a guy who was pawing at her breasts. The curve of his strong jaw reminded her of Jeffrey. He was somewhere in his mid-20s, and his tight black tee shirt showed off his gym-buffed arms and chest, muscles as flashy as any peacock's tail. But he was so drunk that Mira doubted he could stand on his own. She wrinkled her nose at the stink of beer and dance club sweat.

"What's this about?" she asked Rachel.

"I brought him for you!" Rachel beamed. "He's a perfect complement to your genetics!"

"Uh." Mira watched the guy twist Mira's nipples like he was trying to tune an old-fashioned radio. "That's...very thoughtful of you, but...no."

"Why not?" Rachel frowned, clearly perplexed.

"Baby, look at him...he's fifteen years younger than me and sloppy drunk."

The young man lifted his head from Rachel's chest and ogled Mira with bloodshot eyes. "Ahmna drunk, juss alil tipsy."

"If you're worried about his performance, he's had an erection for over an hour."

"I'm...sure he has." Mira bit her lip, trying to figure out how she could gracefully get the young man out of her house.

"Go on," Rachel pulled the young man's hands off her and pushed him toward her mistress. "Go say hello to Mira. She likes you."

He staggered forward like an oversized toddler, grinning. Mira took a step back.

"Izziss gonna be a threeshome?—"

He took another wobbly step, but then his knees buckled and he pitched forward, slamming his forehead into the corner of the marble-topped console table Jeffrey had bought Mira soon after they married.

"Oops," said Rachel.

Mira held Rachel's hand as the paramedics carried the unconscious young man to the ambulance, blue anti-hemorrhage foam mounded on the gash on his face and a brace strapped to his neck. They told her the young man would be fine after he got hospital treatment. Jeffrey was still obliviously coding on the couch.

"Don't worry, I'll clean all the blood off the floor." Rachel sighed. "So sad. He was a perfect genetic match for you."

"I'm sure he was," Mira replied slowly. This was surely the most mortifying thing that had happened to her all year, but she still found herself oddly touched by Rachel's efforts. "I...appreciate what you tried to do. But please don't bring me any more guys."

"How can you get pregnant without one? You told me artificial insemination is too expensive, and he would have been free!"

"Oh, Rachel."

Mira paused. The android *did* have a valid point. She certainly wasn't going to magically conceive all by herself. If she ever developed a super power, parthenogenesis wasn't likely to be it.

"There are some things I can try on my own that will be less...awkward," Mira finally said. "Hopefully."

"All right." Rachel sounded cheerfully skeptical. "Whatever you think is best. But let me see the men, okay? I want you to have a good baby."

"I will."

Mira decided to set up a profile on HeckYesDates. Further, she decided she'd be completely honest in her introductory hologram and tell her prospective suitors that not only was she looking someone to father her child, her android would be chaperoning all first meetings.

The replies didn't exactly flood her account. And when they gradually trickled in over the course of the next few weeks, she was fairly appalled at her prospective suitors. The first guy was dressed in black tactical gear and ranted about racial purity. The second rambled about playgrounds and was visibly high on drugs. The third could barely string any words together at all and at one point he drooled on himself. Her mood sank lower and lower; surely this terrible dating site was no more than a one-way ticket to Loserville.

But her hope began to bloom again when she received a reply from a fourth respondent. He was a man in his late 30s, and he seemed witty and intelligent and wasn't bad looking. Mira showed his hologram to Rachel, who walked all around his image, staring at it as if she were evaluating a used car.

"Look at his fingers. He's got webbing." The android shook her head. "He's genetically risky."

"Oh." Mira was crestfallen. She'd been so taken with his green eyes and Dr. Seuss quotes that she hadn't noticed his hands, which he mostly held behind his back during his monologue.

"I'm going back to the bars," Rachel announced. "I will do my best to find a sober man."

"Fine." Mira was too tired to argue.

Three hours later, Rachel came through the front door with a sleeping baby wrapped in a pink blanket. The android was smiling widely, clearly pleased with herself.

"Oh, you didn't!" Mira was aghast.

Rachel's smile fell from her face. "I—"

"No. I don't want to hear it." The infant wasn't hers, *couldn't* be hers, and to let her think for even just an instant that she could keep this baby...no. It was just cruel. Crueler than any of Jeffrey's rejections. It was as cruel as a drone strike. "Whatever you did, you're undoing it, right now."

"But—"

"No, Rachel. Goddamn it, *no*." Mira couldn't even bring herself to look at the infant's face. She felt tears rise in her eyes, and she forced herself to think of the cold practicalities of the situation. The parents would be frantic; they had to return the baby to her family as soon as possible if she hoped to avoid a kidnapping charge. "You can't just steal a baby. You *can't.* You're taking her back. Show me where you got her. *Right now.*"

Furiously miserable, Mira led the android out into the darkened neighborhood and they got in Jeffrey's car. Rachel sang a quiet lullaby to the child as they drove four miles south through winding side streets until they reached a cul-de-sac that was filled with fire trucks and emergency vehicles. Orange flames engulfed the wreck of a bombed-out two-story house.

Mira just stared at the fire for a moment, her anger melting into horror. "Did the baby...?"

"She came from there, yes. I was heading to a club nearby when I heard the drone hit. I'm programmed to help if I can in emergencies. I got here first. The remaining structure had only just started burning. The mother came out, handed me her baby, and told me to take her someplace safe. She went back inside for her other children and never came back out."

Rachel gazed at Mira. "I did what she wanted. I took her baby someplace safe."

Mira shook her head, simultaneously wanting to weep at the deaths of the other children and trying to tamp down her hope that this surviving baby might be hers now. No. She couldn't be this fortunate in the face of someone else's disaster. It wasn't right. "Her relatives will be looking for her. She'll be missed."

"No, she won't." Rachel tapped her forehead. "I looked up the family. The parents were both second-generation only children. They have no extended family. If you don't take this baby, she will end up in the foster care."

The overburdened foster system in their city ate babies alive and spat out youthful criminals with PTSD. But who was Mira kidding? Her ticking hormones weren't a substitute for good parenting skills. On the other hand, she had Rachel, and the android might count for a whole lot.

"But...but we don't have a birth certificate, or adoption papers," Mira said. "We'll need documentation for her to see a doctor and go to school."

"All electronic," Rachel replied. "I know that Jeffrey broke into the Juno database and reassigned my serial number to you. Those systems are well-protected, so I expect he could also break into the state adoption systems, or find someone else who can."

Rachel handed the swaddled, still-sleeping infant over to Mira, who held her close, feeling her heart ache at the smell of talcum powder and baby. She didn't even try to blink back the tears streaming down her face. Gazing down at the sleeping child for the first time, she vowed to herself that she would be the best mother she could possibly be. She'd make Jeffrey unplug and get counseling. She'd go on antidepressants. Nothing could be perfect, she knew, but whatever it took, she'd make things right for this little girl.

"Her name is Belinda," Rachel offered.

"Thank you," was all Mira could say.

Approaching Lavender

Rhetta's husband Scott teased her for bringing her sketchpad along on their honeymoon: "I thought this was supposed to be just you and me. Not you, me and your *hobby*."

She felt heat rise in her sunburned face at his ha-ha-only-serious tone. It wasn't a hobby, and he knew that. Or she'd thought he did. He'd never complained about her working on her art when they were dating. He'd praised her paintings and cheerfully accompanied her to gallery hops and art shows. It had even been his idea to stop to see the Van Goghs at the museum when they drove through Cincinnati.

"I wanted to get some details of the ocean and the palm trees," she replied.

He waved a cheap digital camera at her. The lens was smeared with sunscreen. "That's why we have this. Put that down and let's go get some margaritas."

A month after they returned from Cancun, he started complaining about her spending her evenings at the studio.

"I never see you," he said. "A wife should be home with her husband. Not off someplace playing with crayons."

She paused, staring at him. He certainly *looked* like the man she'd dated: the same soulful brown eyes, the same tidy blond beard, the same scar on his cheek from when he fell off his bike as a kid. But that was not a sentence she'd ever expected to come out of his mouth. What had changed? Or had *anything* changed? Had she just been oblivious to what he really thought of her passion?

"People are expecting illustrations from me. I have to work—"

He made a dismissive noise. "All that's just a hobby. Your work is at the insurance company."

She wanted to slap him and shout *What is wrong with you?* but her hand stayed perfectly still at her side. "I have contracts. They're paying me. Some of them have already paid. My *work* is expected, and I need to finish it."

"It's hardly any money, though, is it? Just pocket change. Barely anything compared to what you make at the company. Or *could* make if you'd just apply yourself there for a change."

He sounded just like his father, who'd given him almost the same dressing-down when they'd visited for Christmas. Apparently, Scott's desire to stay in accounting wasn't good enough for Mr. Bershung. His father demanded to know why Scott wasn't on track to become a company executive and turned brutally scornful when Scott insisted he was happy where he was.

Her head spun. Scott had been miserable and frustrated after his father's lecture; why would he say the same thing to her? She'd spent whole evenings talking about her dreams of being a full-time artist, and how the tech writing job was just something to bring in a little cash until she started landing better commissions. Scott had nodded and said *I'm sure you'll do it* and other such supportive things. He'd never cared about her making money. Or had he, and she didn't remember it?

"I'd make more money at my art if I didn't have the day job," she said. "And I could get everything done during the day. I could spend all evening with you. We could go out on dates—"

"No." He shook his head, frowning like she'd just suggested they move to the bad side of town. "You can't quit your job. We need the money too much."

"But if I had more time to work—"

"It's a pipe dream to think you'd ever make anything close to a respectable living as an artist. And that studio space is too expensive. It's at least as much as the cable bill."

"Why? Why do we need so much money? We're doing fine."

"No, we're *not* fine." He turned on her, his face turned dark red; she was afraid he'd start throwing something. She'd only seen him that angry once before after someone keyed his brand-new BMW, and she didn't want to see him like that again.

He took a breath, and seemed a few degrees calmer. "We need to save as much as we can for the house."

"House?" Her voice was a dry croak. She was sure the apartment floor would give way beneath her feet at any moment. She wracked her memory. He'd never even mentioned wanting a house, much less that they had some plan to get one. "What house?"

"My parents' place." He fiddled with his Rolex impatiently. "They're getting a condo down in Florida next year. I offered to buy their house from them; dad wants market price, $500K, and it needs a lot of work, but it's structurally sound—"

"And when were you going to talk to me about this?" She'd been in his parents' house only once for the uncomfortable Christmas where he and his father argued about Scott's career. The huge place was all dark wood and shrouded windows and furnishings from the 1950s. Lots of space and some lovely views from the porch, but on the whole she found it oppressive. Even more oppressive was Scott's father: Mr. Bershung was a stern relic from an earlier era, and with his thick accent and ramrod-stiff bearing she imagined him as a sword-brandishing Prussian general. Very little about Rhetta appeared to please Scott's father. She got along much better with his mother, but the old lady seemed unable to do much besides mouth friendly platitudes and offer cookies. Conversation was a lost art in that house.

"What's to talk about?" Scott stared down at her. "We're married now and we need a house."

It was a done deal to him, clearly, and her opinion wasn't required. She twisted her wedding ring around on her finger and scanned the room, hoping to see the glint of a hidden camera or some other indication that this was just a sick prank involving secret twins or pod people. *We've secretly replaced this woman's husband with an utter jerk. Let's see if she notices!* She flashed back on the Hollywood marriage of a starlet to a country singer; a month in, the starlet had demanded divorce on the grounds of "fraud." At the time, Rhetta had wondered what could possibly constitute fraud in a marriage. Now she was starting to get the idea.

But she wasn't a starlet who could marshal her lawyers and file papers a mere month after her wedding. She made a commitment, 'til death did they part, and she believed in her vows. There *had* to be a way to make this work the way it was supposed to.

"I think what we need," she replied slowly, "is to see a marriage counselor."

*

Dr. Gates was a pleasant man in his late 50s and came highly recommended on the insurance company's website. His office was outfitted in plush brown leather couches and expensive silk plants. A bright purple Siamese fighting fish drifted in a glass bowl on his desk. An oil portrait of a woman about his age was on the wall behind his desk; Rhetta guessed it was Mrs. Gates. The woman in the portrait was dressed in a pink cashmere sweater and gazed adoringly at a baby in her arms, the very picture of a perfect grandmother. Rhetta was impressed by the colors and the artist's technique; the painting was more life-like than most photos she'd seen.

Rhetta and Scott took the couch closest to the door and Dr. Gates sat across from them in a brown plastic folding chair, listening intently as they both told their stories. When they were done, he leaned forward sympathetically.

"This is exactly the kind of situation that leads to annulments," the kindly therapist said. "I firmly believe that marriage is not something to be entered into or exited lightly, so I'm extremely glad you two came to see me. I think we can get things back on the right track here."

He turned toward her husband. "Scott, it seems to me that you came into this marriage with regimented gender role expectations that you failed to convey to your wife, certainly before your wedding, but also after it."

"Anything's possible," Scott replied.

Dr. Gates seemingly ignored his skeptical tone. "I'd like to see you make space for your wife's aspirations and most particularly her art. If you want her at home and don't want to pay for studio space, then you need to make room for her whole life at your home. And you need to fully include her in decisions that involve her. And *everything* involves her now."

Scott slumped in his chair, fiddling with his watch.

"Spouses are life partners," the therapist said. "You need to help her become the best possible person she can be."

It seemed to Rhetta that something clicked behind her husband's eyes. He straightened up and smiled. "If you put it that way…of course I want her to be the best wife ever."

"Person," Dr. Gates corrected.

"Sure," replied Scott.

The therapist turned to Rhetta. "And I'd like to see you try to be a genuine partner to your husband."

"I thought I have been," she replied. "I work a job I don't especially enjoy for the sake of financial goals that are his and not mine."

"Now, Rhetta," the therapist admonished gently. "Everyone has to make a living, and it's not Scott's fault you've chosen a job that doesn't entirely suit you, is it? I respect your art—clearly you are quite talented from what I've heard—but that, too, is a choice. And it's a choice that's been causing your husband some discomfort."

She felt a slow crab of panic start to scrabble in the pit of her stomach. She could no more choose to stop painting and drawing than she could choose to stop eating. Her soul would dry up.

"So the problem in your view is that I have choices?" she asked.

The therapist smiled in an irritated way. "The problem is that you've been insensitive to your husband's needs for comfort and routine. He's clearly a very traditional man, and I find it hard to believe that after two years of dating you were unaware of that."

She crossed her arms. "I told you already. He hid that part of himself."

Inside, she had to agree with Dr. Gates: it did seem impossible that she hadn't seen that side of him. Sure, Scott's father was a domineering tyrant who wanted his wife to serve him coffee every day in exactly the same mug at 7am sharp, but her boyfriend had never been like that at all. The man she knew from two years of dating had been attentive, kind, sexy, spontaneous, and most important, he talked to her. The most perfect of perfect catches, everyone agreed. He'd had a chivalrous streak she found a little old-fashioned and endearing in a world of oblivious hipsters who were often more interested in their video games than they were in her. Most guys had made her feel like she rated only slightly higher than a Fleshlight, but Scott was never indifferent. He'd never failed to make her feel special. Was that the secret-tip off? He'd held open doors and pulled out chairs and mostly bought dinner; was all that her cue that some strange switch was going to flip after the rings were on and he'd start turning into a clone of the old man? She couldn't believe it.

Dr. Gates broke her from her reverie: "You need to be more sensitive to his needs. If he makes space for you at home, will you stay home to paint?"

"Well, of course."

"And would it kill you to cook?" the therapist asked, his tone joking. *Ha-ha, only serious.*

She had to struggle to keep her hand tucked under her elbow. "I. Already. Do."

"But only a few times a week, right? Takeout and frozen dinners make him feel unloved."

"It was his idea to get Chinese takeout once a week. And he could cook, too."

"Now, Rhetta. This is about partnership. He has considerably more job responsibilities than you do, and it's only fair that you take over more of the household duties."

Rhetta thought about asking the therapist to do the math on how much work she did between her day job and the freelance, but she bit back that reply. Apparently her career was a choice, and his was a hero's quest. "Fine. I'll cook."

"Then it's settled." Dr. Gates smiled at her, then at Scott. "Be sure to give your father my best."

"I will," her husband replied.

Scott gave up the walk-in closet in the hallway. It was just big enough for her chair, an easel, a stand for her laptop and Wacom tablet, plus a few bins of supplies. She replaced the sallow overhead light with a bulb that emitted a natural spectrum. A room with a window would have been better, but at least she finally had her own private space in the apartment. She lined the beige walls with her art and made do. It felt a little too much like a cell, and there wasn't enough air circulation for her to use oils or acrylics without feeling woozy, but she was able to immerse herself in the pencil lines and digital paint strokes and got her commissioned pieces done on time.

But her new schedule got harder and harder to maintain. She had to be up by 6 to catch the bus to work, and after work she immediately got to work on their dinner and chores. Afterward, Scott would want her to keep him company while he watched his favorite sitcoms. Sometimes it was 9 or 10 before she got to work in her art closet. Most nights she was up until 1 or 2 in the morning.

The constant low-grade sleep deprivation started taking its toll. She missed her bus a few times and was late to her job, and on a couple of embarrassing situations she fell asleep in long meetings. One day her boss called her into his office and told her she was on probation for three months and would be fired if her job performance didn't improve.

In her gut, she knew nothing good could come of telling Scott about what happened, but decided it would be fundamentally bad for their relationship if she started keeping secrets.

"You better not lose your job!" His tone was an unpleasant echo of his father's Christmas lecturing. "I can't have you unemployed and lounging around the house all day. We need the money for the house."

"I wouldn't be lounging; I made $1000 on commissions just last month—" she began, but he'd already turned on his heel and marched off to the living room.

The next day, he surprised her with a wrapped box when she got home.

"I realized I acted like a real jerk yesterday, and I'm sorry," he said. "Your happiness is important to me, so I got you this."

She opened the box, and inside she found a new set of red-shellacked brushes and shiny tin tubes of paint. The mink, hog, and badger hair brushes were handmade, and the paints bore hand-inked German labels. She didn't recognize the maker's mark. The whole set had the aura of an expensive boutique.

"Wow. Thank you, honey." She blinked down at the set in pleased confusion. "They're lovely. Where did you find them?"

"My father told me where to get them. A special order from Europe. He commissioned a portrait of my mother a few months after they married, and the artist he hired used the same kind of brushes and paints. They were going through a kind of a rough patch at first, and he said the painting really helped her perspective."

Rhetta was pretty sure there hadn't been any paintings in his parents' house at all aside from a couple of art fair landscapes. "Have I seen that one?"

"Oh, no. My father keeps it in his study behind little curtains. Even I haven't seen it; I think he had her pose nude." He cleared his throat, clearly a bit uncomfortable at the thought of actually seeing the artwork. "But these paints have the best colors in the world."

"If you haven't seen your mom's portrait, how do you know that?"

"He got an artist to do a picture of me—I saw it when I went up there a couple of weekends ago. My dad originally planned to have both of us painted for a wedding present, but they couldn't find a good photo of you for the artist without asking me and ruining the surprise, so they decided to just do me. And then my parents decided they liked it so much they wanted to keep it. It's in the foyer; you'll see it next time we visit. It's an amazing portrait; the artist did me as a big-shot CEO. It's like I look at it and I can see my future."

He paused, his eyes shining. "I know you can't paint in the closet because of the fumes, so I thought you could set your easel up in the living room."

She blinked at him. "Really?"

He smiled. "Just one condition."

The panic crab shuddered in her stomach. "What?"

"I want you to make *me* a painting for a change. I want you to put aside all that stuff you're doing for strangers and create a portrait of yourself that I'll feel proud to hang in my office. I want to show the world what a beautiful, talented wife I have. Can you do that for me?"

She was touched at his interest, and she couldn't think of a single reason to object. "Sure, honey, I can do that."

He drove her down to Dick Blick's and together they picked out an oil-primed stretched linen canvas.

"Oh, this will be just the right size to go between my bookshelves!" he exclaimed, holding the 30"x30" canvas up against an imaginary wall in the middle of the aisle.

His enthusiasm was contagious. She smiled. "I'll try to get it done as soon as possible."

"No." He set down the canvas and took both her hands in his, gazing down at her intently. "I want you to take your time with this. I want your very best. I want to be the envy of the entire accounting firm."

The crab stirred inside her, but she didn't know why. She set her fear aside as unreasonable, maybe hormones or the weather. And she made herself smile. "Absolutely, honey. I'll give you my very best."

"That's my girl." He planted a kiss on her forehead.

When they got home, she emailed her clients to get a few weeks extension on her projects, and then she put down a small drop cloth and set the easel atop it in the living room beside the sofa. She started lightly sketching in details with a soft graphite pencil.

"What's that in your hands?" Scott squinted at the sketch.

"Brushes and pastel pencils," she replied.

"I don't like those. Why don't you put in some lavender?"

She paused. "I'm allergic to lavender."

"So? You don't actually have to hold it to paint it, do you? Lavender's pretty. I like it."

Portraying herself holding something she couldn't even be in the same room with violated the fundamental truth of the art, but it also didn't seem worth arguing about. She decided she'd treat her husband like any other client and give him what he wanted. This wouldn't be a self-portrait; it would be a painting of an idealized woman who happened to look a lot like her.

"Okay, lavender it is."

With Scott looking over her shoulder during the sketching, the planned color scheme ended up with a lot more pinks and purples than would have been her choice. She wanted to show herself in her favorite gray sweater; he wanted her in a pale pink suit jacket and cream-colored blouse. Rhetta was able to find some reference photos on the Ann Taylor website. She wanted to leave her lips natural; he asked for ruby red lipstick. Most everything ended up being a shade or two different than she would have chosen for herself.

The next evening, she peeled off the thin foils sealing the paint tubes. The paints had an odd organic smell unlike any other oil paints she'd used. It had a strongly spicy odor; she smelled cloves and lemongrass, and maybe catnip? A touch of licorice or absinthe? Beneath the spice, there was a slight stench of rot.

Maybe the paint maker had used animal fats that had started to turn? But who would use an oil that could go rancid?

Rhetta squeezed paints into the wells on her palette and began to mix them. The thick colors flowed together wonderfully. There was no sign the paints had spoiled. She picked out a badger filbert brush and began work on her jacket.

The shaft of the wooden brush was surprisingly cold in her hand; she could almost imagine it was a chilled steel rod except it wasn't nearly heavy enough. As she worked, the cold seemed to seep into the bones of her hand and up into her wrist.

"Everything all right, honey?" Scott asked.

"It's…yes." She rubbed her wrist. "Is it cold in here?"

"Maybe a little; I'll go get you a wrap."

The afghan he brought down did little to keep her warm, and when she was done with her work for the evening, she felt exhausted and shuddered with chills. She knew she couldn't afford to call in sick now that she was on probation, so she took some echinacea and put herself right to bed. At least she'd made pretty good progress on the painting; all the shapes and colors were roughed in, and she could start work on the details the next night.

The next morning, she woke in a groggy panic, realizing she'd slept through her alarm. Scott was already gone. She washed up at the sink and dressed as quickly as she could, praying that the second bus would be early for a change and that traffic through downtown would be light. The drive was pure agony; every tick of the clock made her feel like an accused witch being pressed under an enormous stone by inquisitors.

The bus was slow. Traffic was harsh. She got to work fifteen minutes late. Nearly in tears, she hurried up the stairs, trying to think of anything she could say to her supervisor to save her job—

"Oh, good, you're back." Her supervisor smiled at her and handed her a thick stack of printouts. "I need these proofed by 3pm."

"Yes, sir." Her hands shook as she took the papers.

He noticed her trembling. "Everything okay?"

"Yes. I…I just got startled on the stairwell."

"All right." He looked her up and down, frowning slightly at her khakis and blue polo. "Were you wearing a different outfit earlier?"

She shook her head, her mouth dry. "No, sir."

"Huh. Must have been a trick of the light. Talk to you later."

Holding the papers to her chest, Rhetta stepped down the cubicle aisle to her gray-walled cell. The keyboard tray was pulled out and her computer was on, the screensaver locked. She set the papers down and unlocked her machine.

A Word document was open, and the cursor bar flashed at the end of a single line:

Finish the portrait.

The sudden smell of lavender crept up her nostrils, and Rhetta sneezed. Dabbing her runny nose with a Kleenex, she looked to the right of her computer. A single stalk of dried lavender lay on her desk. She quickly wrapped it in a plastic bag from her desk drawer and stuck the offending flowers in the trash.

The panic crab squeezed her lungs, and she couldn't seem to get her breath for a moment. Who had broken into her computer and left the lavender? And how did he know about the painting? What was going on?

Rhetta turned to the documentation contractor across the aisle and waved nervously to get his attention.

He pulled his earbuds out. "What's up?"

"Was tech support working on my computer this morning?" Rhetta asked.

"I didn't see them. But you were here before me, so I'm maybe not the person to ask."

It took Rhetta a moment to get more words out. "I…you got here *after* I did?"

"Oh, definitely." He nodded.

"When?"

"Like, I dunno…I cut it pretty close this morning! Like maybe 7:55 or something."

Rhetta thought she might faint. "Okay, thanks."

She turned back to her computer and the cryptic sentence. It didn't make sense. She *knew* she'd just gotten into the office, fifteen minutes late. Was her coworker in on some weird prank people were playing on her? What in the hell was going on?

The building anxiety turned her bowels to liquid, so she got up to go to the ladies' room. When she pushed through the door, she came face-to-face with what she first thought was a newly-installed full-length wall mirror. And then she realized it was a flesh-and-blood woman staring back at her. A woman who looked almost exactly like her, except her double had ruby-red lipstick and wore a stylish pale purple blouse and matching slacks. Her perfume smelled like lavender.

The woman's eerie face twisted into a scowl. "I told you to go finish the portrait!"

She slapped Rhetta across her cheek, hard, and when her palm connected it felt like she'd been hit with a taser. The electric shock made her vision go white, and she felt herself drop to the tiled floor.

Rhetta came awake in her chair in the living room, a chilly brush in her hand, the afghan draped across her shoulders. The portrait before her was nearly complete; all that was missing were some of the details on her face and in the lavender flowers.

"That is looking *so wonderful*, honey." Scott leaned down and kissed the top of her head. "I'm so proud of you."

"I…think I'm done for the evening." Her voice shook.

"You can finish it tomorrow."

He helped her clean her brushes, then took her upstairs and they went to bed. Once she was sure he was asleep, she crept out of bed, put on her favorite comfy warmup suit to combat the chill in her core, and went back down to the living room.

Rhetta stopped a yard from the painting and stared at it, afraid to touch it. Whatever was going on, the painting was at the center of it; she could feel it in her bones. She couldn't finish it. She had to make it go away. Cut it up. Bury it. Burn it.

"No," said a voice to her right. Her voice. The lavender double's voice.

Rhetta ducked and raised a hand to ward off another stunning blow, but the doppelganger tackled her instead. They landed on the couch, the double pressing her down into the cushions with its surprising strength. The smell of lavender was nearly overpowering; it was hard to breathe through the flowery stench. How much had the creature already drained from her?

"You'll finish it," growled the doppelganger. Its breath smelled rancid like the undertones in the paints. Rhetta felt an electric prickling where its bare flesh touched hers.

"No, I won't!"

"You're nothing but a lefthanded version of me. You'll do as I say." The doppelganger pried Rhetta's mouth open with hard fingers and pressed its lips to hers. The shock was intense but not enough to completely stupefy her.

The doppelganger's fingers stayed vises but the rest of its flesh turned to a foul gel. It started vomiting itself into the artist. The fluid was greasy and bitter with turpentine, poisonous herbs and heavy metals. Rhetta fought, to no avail; the doppelganger flowed into her, filling her throat and stomach and guts, seeping out into her veins and muscles.

Rhetta felt as though she was being worn like a tight suit. She felt her legs lift her body and walk her to the painting; she saw her hands uncover the palette and pick up the damp, cold brushes.

She shut her eyes, hoping that would confound the doppelganger. It did not. She felt the friction of the bristles on the canvas through the frigid shaft.

"It is finished," the doppelganger announced in her own voice. "And so are you."

It marched her out into the dark back yard, knelt beside a pile of autumn leaves, and stuck a finger down her throat.

This time, it was Rhetta's essence carried on the bitter purge. She found herself vomited from her own body, melting helplessly into the parched rakings.

"There." The doppelganger straightened up. It frowned down at the old warmup suit it wore, then stripped it off and unceremoniously dumped it beside the leaves. "An important man's wife would never wear something as frumpy this!"

The doppelganger strode back to the house and shut the door.

Rhetta dried up in the leaves in the moonlight, blind, voiceless, bodiless, but she could still feel everything.

A little after midnight, a wind rose, stirred the leaves, and carried her away into the forgotten places in the night.

Dura Mater

COMMLOGWALKERDEBORAH00012122054001

Dear Mom,

I'm sorry I won't be there for Christmas, and I'm sorry I left without explaining everything to you, but...I signed onto the Kepler colony mission. It was an opportunity I just couldn't pass up. They were looking for civilians with certain tech skills—I have 'em because of my coding and quantum networking background—and they're paying a *ridiculous* amount of money.

Andres has been sick with worry about little Marilu's brain tumor and the bills, and...I just made the bills go away! She'll be talking by the time I get back, but she *will* be talking, and walking, and my little brother won't be bankrupt. I hope that's worth a couple of missed Christmases.

It's a four-day shuttle flight to the hyperspace portal, and then I'll be onboard the *Joliet.* We'll be in hyperspace for a year, going a hundred times faster than the speed of light. I'll send messages and (fingers crossed that the tech works right) you should get at least the first ones over the next few months. They'll arrive less frequently as I get further out. I'll be home before the last ones ever reach you! But we won't be able to receive transmissions once we jump; I'm part of the team working on that problem. It's a tricky thing getting planet-based quantum communicators to link to a ship that's slipped outside normal spacetime. Being one of the people who figures that out would be *huge.*

So, please let me know you got this, and I'll write you again soon.

Love,

Deb

COMMLOGWALKERDEBORAH00012142054001

Hi Mom,

I was really glad to get your message. I know you have a lot of questions, and I know you're worried, but really, it'll be okay.

First off, the *Bartolomé* disintegrated because of a crack in the engines, not because of a portal malfunction. It was a terrible thing, but they've taken every possible precaution to keep that from happening again.

And second, you're totally right: the first bunch of ships to Kepler carried everyone in hibernation pods. Everything was automated, and all that worked just fine. They don't *need* live crews working these ships...and that's a big part of why my crew is traveling this way. They don't know how hyperspace affects people who are awake and working onboard these ships. Eventually they *will* need live crews, so they need our data. So yes, I'm going to be a guinea pig. Which is why my paycheck is so ridiculous!

Third, this has nothing to do with Mark and Sofia. That was five years ago, and I've moved on. This is me still moving on.

And finally, I won't be gone for ten years. My contract calls for a year out, a year working on-site, and a year back, probably in a hibernation pod unless they need more data. So it's just three years; I'll be home before you know it. Heck, I'll be back before *I* know it; they're saying a year in hyperspace will feel like just three or four months, but again, that's something they're still gathering data on.

So: it'll be fine. Give that niece of mine extra kisses and hugs for me when you see her, okay? And I guess if you can spare 'em, one or two for her daddy and Papa, too. <g>

Love,

Deb

COMMLOGWALKERDEBORAH00012182054001

Hi Mom,

We are underway! The jump to hyperspace went off without a hitch yesterday morning. And in even better news, I was able to finally keep some food down this afternoon. <g>

We all went through hours and hours of hyperspace simulation, but honestly the sims were nothing like the real thing. It's so...*weird.* It's not just being mostly weightless—I got used to that on the shuttle ride over. It's...everything's just *off.* It's like I don't know where my own body is anymore, and I keep fumbling around. I have no idea what time it is; if we didn't have clocks none of us would have a clue. I'm dizzy and nauseated. It feels less like motion sickness and more like being hooked up to a mild electric current. Our medical team swears all that will get better after a few days, and I hope so; meanwhile, they're going through just as many airsick bags as we are.

We have windows on the observation deck so we can see out into hyperspace. And in its own way, it's the weirdest part of the whole thing. At first you think it's this expanse of blackness, just like regular space, only you can't see any stars. But then the longer you stare out into it...you start to realize you don't know *what* color it really is. It's a color, all right, but not something any human being ever evolved to perceive. One guy, a medical researcher named Vince, gave himself a full-on panic attack staring out at it. Doctor's orders? Don't look out the windows more than five minutes. And I'm just fine with that.

Love,

Deb

COMMLOGWALKERDEBORAH00012252054001

Hi Mom,

Merry Christmas! I'm picturing you all at the table eating goose and Aunt Ximena's tamales. Thanks to something Dr. Cedar cooked up, we're all over being hyperspace-sick and had turkey and ham for dinner. It really wasn't half bad, although I'm pretty sure it was all soy (I spent a lot of time outgassing in the head afterward).

We had a holiday exchange; the stowage limits were pretty strict, but they told us to bring something light and fun. Team building! So I wrapped a couple of bars of gourmet chocolate in snowflake hologram paper, and I got a pair of little bottles of Grand Marnier from Vince, he of the window panic attack I mentioned.

Mark loved Grand Marnier. The last time I'd had any was at his wake. Funny how the taste and smell of something can bring so many memories flooding back, isn't it? I couldn't sleep after the party, and I ended up in the hibernation pod racks staring down at the face of this little colonist girl who looks so much like Sofia. I just started sobbing.

Vince found me back there and talked to me a while. Turns out he's from Ohio; his folks have a rice farm. He lost his wife in the Lake Shore Bullet Train crash seven years ago; she was pregnant with their first child. He misses her so much, and it's obvious he still loves her more than anything. I feel for the guy. It was good talking to him, though.

Probably most of the crewmembers have their own heartaches. All of us live long enough, we lose someone we don't want to live without, but we have to keep going anyhow.

Love to all of you. Make sure you're hugging my niece! Can't get too many hugs at her age.

Deb

COMMLOGWALKERDEBORAH00001012055001

Hay Ma!

Hhaspy New Yaer! Hope ur having a gret time! Engneering made a still and whooooa thts some stron stuff!

Vinse sez he cn seee ghosts out th wijndows. Hes such a bobo!

Looooovvvvvvveeee

DEB!

COMMLOGWALKERDEBORAH00001012055002

Hi Mom,

I'm really sorry for the drunk message I sent. I haven't been that hammered in my life. Not as hung over as I expected; Dr. Cedar was handing out a remedy last night and it seems to have worked. But the dizziness is worse than ever, so I'm staying strapped in my bunk for a while.

I wanted to come clean with you about something. When I told you that I wasn't doing this because of Mark and Sofia? That was a pathetic and obvious lie. I kept hoping that if I told it to myself enough times, it would become true.

Have you ever been so sad and missed someone so badly that you thought your heart surely would stop? And yet, it never does? I feel hollow inside, and angry at God for taking them away from me. With all the medical advances we have, why do people still die from the flu? And I brought it home to them, God damn it. In my nightmares I see them in the ICU. Especially Sofia. Watching her struggle to breathe like that, fight and suffer and die anyhow...Jesus, that tore me up in a way I'll never get over. I know it about killed you and Papa too.

The first year I thought, okay, I'm mourning, I'll get over it. But I never did. If I see something that makes me smile, I'll turn to tell Mark about it...and of course he's not there. I'll do that three, four times a day. I'll walk down the street and hear a baby laugh and I'll look for Sofia...and suddenly in my mind I'm watching her die all over again.

And I still love Mark. I've tried dating, I really have. I want my family back, I want to try for another baby, but...I just can't make it work. I can't bring myself to fake it for someone I don't care about. As bad as I still want to be a mother, I just can't get past wanting Mark, and there's no way I can ever have him again.

A few months ago, I realized that the whole wide beautiful world is full of constant reminders of him and Sofia, and the ten thousandth time waking up and realizing they're gone doesn't hurt any less than the first and second.

Solution? Get off the world.

So now I'm somewhere far beyond the solar system traveling 20 million miles per second...and there are still sleeping beauties and tiny bottles of Grand Marnier out here.

But it's a whole new year, and something has to change.

Love,

Deb

COMMLOGWALKERDEBORAH000000000000001

Dear Mom,

We hit something. Nobody knows what or how. The whole ship rattled around like a carnival ride and I got slammed into a bulkhead. I'm fine but don't know how long I was unconscious. It looks like all the auxiliary power went out for a while. But we're still in hyperspace, and all the hibernation pods seem fine, and the nav computer looks okay, but...something's not right with the clocks. We have two atomic clocks onboard, and they should be synched perfectly but they're off by months. There should be no way that could ever happen. Nobody knows what it means. On past flights, they found some discrepancies in atomic clocks kept in different parts of the ships, but we're talking milliseconds there.

The other thing is, I'm getting an error every time I try to access my sent messages, so I have no idea if the system is transmitting properly or not. Another thing we have to troubleshoot. My head really hurts.

More later; Vince is having another panic attack I think. He is screaming complete nonsense. I better go see if I can help.

Love,

Deb

COMMLOGWALKERDEBORAH000000000000002

Dear Mom,

Vince nearly killed himself; he may still die. Dr. Cedar sedated him and we locked him in an observation room. But he woke up screaming and gouged his own eyes out with his fingers and started tearing his face off. He did a lot of damage to himself before they were able to sedate him again. He's tied down now, his face covered in blood-soaked bandages.

He's such a sweet guy. It's so terrible what's happened to him, but it's especially hard on his wife Rufina. She told me she's expecting their first baby.

More later.

Love,

Deb

COMMLOGWALKERDEBORAH000000000000003

Dear Mom,

I found Dr. Cedar dead in the hall outside sickbay. I can't get her face out of her mind. She looked like she'd been dead a month; she was all dried out and her lips were pulled back from her teeth in a horrible grin. And her eyes—oh God. You would have bad dreams forever so I won't tell you.

Her sister, the other Dr. Cedar, says it was an undiagnosed aneurysm and she was only dead a couple of hours. I don't see how that's possible, but she's the doctor, right?

I'm really glad Mark is here and we're patching things up, finally. I had so many nightmares that he and Sofia got sick and died, but she's safe in her hibernation pod and he's sitting just across the room. I really missed him, Mom.

But...I know I haven't been with him, but...I can't remember why we separated? Or when? I remember the nightmares. But it's been years...or has it? And I feel like Sofia should be...older now? Or is that just the hyperspace affecting my memory?

I wish I could talk to you. I wish I could talk to Vince. I feel like he'd be able to help me sort out what's in my head. At least he's still alive; Dr. Cedar says she thinks he'll pull through, but she has to keep him in a medical coma until we get to Kepler.

We're all still getting error messages when we try to access our message archives; I tracked down a couple of lines of corrupted code yesterday, but fixing them didn't help. If I didn't know better I'd think the damn program had been rewritten.

I wish this headache would go away. Dr. Cedar's meds make me too sleepy and stupid to work.

Love,

Deb

COMMLOGWALKERDEBORAH000000000000004

Dear Mom,

Sorry it's been so long since I wrote you. I had a bad reaction to the drugs we've been taking for hyperspace sickness and came down with meningitis, of all things, but Dr. Cedar is getting me squared away. Finally the headache is getting better. I've been confined to quarters because I can't stand the lights, but Mark's been the best. He's been telling me all about how we're going to give Sofia brothers and sisters soon. He'll be a great dad. I can't wait.

Love,

Deb

COMMLOGWALKERDEBORAH000000000000005

Dear Mom,

Time has flown! But you know how busy it is when you're expecting. I can't believe how pregnant I am right now, and the babies are so active! Mark is one proud papa. He says I am the best mother he's ever seen. Dr. Cedar thinks there are eight babies? They all get wound around each other and it's hard to make them all out on the scanner.

Dr. Cedar and Rufina have been tremendous helps in setting up the nursery. They've spun their silk everywhere; the whole room is so soft and looks like Santa's beard. Vince is in there, and most of the crew from Engineering. They will help the babies get big and strong.

I might not make it through the birth. But I'm okay with that, because my babies will live and that's what's important. It's been so long since the Kthath had a good host species and I could die happy knowing I helped save them. But I don't want you to worry—Mark and Dr. Cedar will do everything they can to make sure I can see them grow up. Mark says I'm tough and I can make it. I have a lot to teach the babies about humans and human behavior so they can fit into the Kepler colony. They'll have to take the places of everyone in the nursery, and that's hard, so I might be gone longer than I said I'd be. But it'll be fine—once my babies have had babies, we'll all head back to Earth.

See you soon,

Deb

The Still-Life Drama of Passing Cars

Co-written with Gary A. Braunbeck

"Mom!" shouted Jason from the back seat of the station wagon. "Lookit that woman! She's crying!"

Tammy Horton caught a glimpse of the shiny black BMW as it sped past. The driver—a woman on the wrong side of forty and trying hard not to look it—was, indeed, crying. Her right hand shook terribly as she wiped at her puffy eyes with a wadded Kleenex, ruined mascara running in dark streaks down both sides of her face. Maybe she was coming from a funeral, or from the hospital where she'd been visiting a dying friend or relative. Or maybe she'd discovered that her husband was having an affair with a younger woman. It didn't matter; the misery on her face and the tears in her eyes told everyone, for just a quick moment shared by passing Monday cars, that her entire world had just collapsed.

"Well?" Tammy asked her children.

Jason and Lynn looked at one another, then Lynn said: "Jason saw it first."

The rules of this particular road game were very strict: If You See It First, You Have To Claim It.

"Okay, Jason…it's yours."

"Cool!"

A moment later he held a dark, wet, squirming mass in his arms.

"Ew!" said Lynn, wrinkling her nose in disgust. "It's uglier than a squid!"

"Want to hold it?"

"Wanna bite me?"

"Knock that off right now, you two." Tammy glanced at the woman in the BMW. There was no longer any soul-crippling sadness on her face; in fact, she looked as if she couldn't quite remember why she'd been so upset.

Tammy changed lanes without bothering to signal. No one sounded their horn. Big surprise. She closed her eyes, knowing she wouldn't crash. When she wasn't able to see the road, she could smell water, and there was a nasty taste like old pond scum in her mouth.

The afternoon sun turned roads and the cars on it into gold.

Tammy's car cast no shadow.

"Mommy!" shouted Lynn, bouncing up and down on the seat beside Jason. "That man over there's hitting his little girl!"

A '76 Impala, its mismatched body panels seemingly held together by rust patches and primer, came up alongside them. The driver—a blond man in his late twenties who had the sunken eyes and hollow cheeks of an alcoholic—repeatedly punched the little girl sitting next to him. He reminded Tammy of her ex-husband. The little girl cowered against the passenger door, trying to ward off the blows by turning her face toward the window. The man was red-faced and screaming, and though Tammy couldn't hear what he was saying, she could tell from the pain on the girl's face that his words hurt much worse than his fist ever could. How many times had the girl been through this? Would she repeat the cycle of abuse with her own children?

The cold lump in the pit of her stomach told Tammy everything she needed to know about the girl's fate. Whether they were victims or perpetrators, those ensnared in violence were destined to relive it. The cycle never ended, not for people like them.

"Your turn, Lynn."

"Got it!"

Lynn turned her attention to a deformed infant on her lap. It made mewling sounds like a kitten. Its head looked like something that floats. Its mouth was a knotted mass of hardened scar tissue. Its eyes were blinded by cataracts.

The man in the other car was staring at his fist in confusion, as if he'd never seen such a thing before; then he reached over and gently caressed the back of the little girl's head. The little girl squirmed and shuddered, then—seeming to forget that Daddy had ever touched in any other way—giggled at something funny the man was saying and leaned her head against his arm.

"Good girl, Lynn," said Tammy, moving the car over into the center lane without signaling.

She pushed in the cigarette lighter, reached down into her battered handbag, and worked a smoke out of what was left of her crushed pack of Virginia Slims. Bending down over her distended belly sent sharp pains through her bladder and lower back. Her ankles were swollen, and her skin was clammy and itchy. *God*, why did she have to be seven months pregnant in the middle of summer?

The lighter popped out. She lit up, taking a deep drag on the cigarette. The smoke tasted sharply foul, like mud and rusty cans. Dammit, every cell in her body craved nicotine; why couldn't the cigs at least taste good, like they used to?

Jason leaned forward, his small face scrunched in a worried frown. "Daddy'll be all mad again. He said—" Tammy coughed as she glanced back at her son. He'd always looked too much like Jake, his father. She forced down her irritation, making herself instead smile. "I love you, hon, 'kay? And I know what your daddy said, but he ain't here no more and we're not gonna be seeing him again for...a while."

"I know," whispered Jason sadly. "I just don't like it when you cough."

"Thank you, hon." Tammy affectionately mussed his hair. He really was a good kid. He'd be a heartbreaker when he grew up. Just like his dad.

She turned her attention back to the road. Her eyes ached and stung from staring at the sun glaring off the endless miles of sunbaked blacktop. She wondered if anyone driving past had taken notice of them on that day three months ago. Had anyone glanced over and said to themselves, "Jesus, that woman looks in bad shape. And those kids! They look like they've not had a good day on this earth since they were born."

Damn Jake. That sonofabitch gave more care to his old Thunderbird than he did to his own family. If he was in a *good* mood, he went off with his buddies and drank himself stupid at the Rusty Nail; when his mood was black and his buddies abandoned him—as was the case more often than not—he raged around their little trailer, cussing and throwing anything he could lay hands on and finding fault with every little goddamn thing everyone said or did and then bringing out the fists if she dared suggested he might help out with the chores and the kids. So he just up and hit the road for Las Vegas in his polished T-bird, taking every last penny they'd saved and not giving a damn that his expectant wife and two other children would soon find themselves broke, evicted, and hungry, with nowhere to go but her old station wagon and no friends or family to call and ask for help....

Did anyone on the highway notice the still-life drama of her family's passing car that day?

She took the usual off-ramp near Lake Gifford, made a left, and drove until she reached the patch of willows and oaks that marked the entrance to the road leading to the fishing dock.

"Already?" groaned her children in unison.

At least they always enjoy the trip, Tammy thought.

"'Fraid so. Put on your seat belts and roll down your windows."

Like the good children they were, Jason and Lynn did as Mommy said.

Tammy floored the accelerator and sped toward the cool, gray-green water.

"I love you," she told her children, trying not to cry this time.

"Love you, too," they replied, always quietly at this part.

The car shot onto the old dock and leapt over the edge, soaring twenty feet before it came down grille-first into the water.

The rest didn't take long.

It never did.

"Mommy!" shouted Jason. "Lookit those old folks in that car. They look happy, don't they?"

Tammy glimpsed the elderly couple as they drove by in a cream-colored Cadillac. They were smiling at each other, looking so very much in love, even after so many, many years.

She both hated and envied them.

Jason tried to Claim It but couldn't.

"I forgot," he said, his voice thick with disappointment. "It can only be the *bad* stuff."

Tammy grunted in pain as she reached down for her never-quite-empty pack of Virginia Slims, lit up and breathed in the muddy, unsatisfying smoke. God, how she hated driving! Her aches seemed worse with every trip, her never-to-be-born baby restless in her womb. Her children laughed and started singing "99 Bottles of Beer on the Wall".

Funny how heaven and hell could work out to be the same thing.

Through Thy Bounty

I stare down at the naked body of the boy on the butcher block as my mother's nightmare washes through me. She is ill. Last night's dreams were filled with fever-warped images of shrouded doctors, knives and needles, tubes and dark blood. The doctors of the Resistance will do their very best for her, but she is an old lady now, her body fragile. The thought that she might die turns my guts to ice.

Her life is my only hope in this Hell. But at least I know she is safe from the Jagaren. For now.

The boy is maybe eight or nine, redheaded, skinny and bruised. His ankles are purple and rope-burned. The gash in his neck is as pale as raw bacon; they've drained the blood from his body. Sometimes, depending on the menu du jour, they leave the chilled blood for me in a stainless steel thermos jug beside the corpse's head. But not today.

He has the look of a child who's been in captivity for a long time. But he has to be the flesh and blood of somebody important in the Resistance, else he would not be here in my kitchen. The Jagaren always have their most precious catches flown in fresh from the battlefield, concentration camp, and torture chamber.

As always, the menu instructions are printed on stiff paper tucked into the corpse's mouth. The Jagaren have been sampling every aspect of Terran cuisine, each day a new ethnic menu. Today they want to taste the Deep South: sweet barbecue, collard greens, chicken fried steak with gravy, chitlins, sausage, watermelon, corn on the cob, fried green tomatoes, and apple pie. Dinner for twelve. I have but eight hours to prepare this meal.

I touch the boy's forehead, close my eyes and say a brief prayer for him. I don't know what religion he had, if any, but we all live under the same God.

Maybe someday He'll remember us. Prayer finished, I pick up my curved knife and begin to skin him.

The boy's left hand has the calluses that come from years of throwing a baseball. A lefty Little League pitcher. As I work, I imagine him playing ball in a sunny Midwestern field, jeans stained with grass and dirt. His grin is the very definition of childhood joy, and he goes home victorious to a hot bath and hugs from his proud father. He spends the evening catching fireflies with his friends until his mother calls him home to be tucked in and read to sleep.

I have been alone here for over a year, all my waking hours spent in this huge, beautiful, damnable kitchen. It has a walk-in refrigerator that is stocked every night as I sleep, an immense pantry of dry goods, racks of jars of dried spices from every corner of the Earth. In case I ever face an unfamiliar menu, the back wall is lined with hundreds of cookbooks selected by the Jagaren; undesirable recipes have been cut out. The side door leads to a room with rows and rows of herbs under grow lights. There's an open-pit barbecue and spit big enough to roast a whole ox, a man-sized oven, wok, industrial meat grinder, and on and on. No kitchen I ever worked in as a chef in Los Angeles and Dallas was even half as well-equipped.

The Jagaren picked their torture well.

I always loved the kitchen, even as a child, and everything I know about cooking, about life, is but a pale shadow of what my mother knows. Her mind, her *will*, is astonishing. When the Jagaren came to take our planet, my mother turned from managing her restaurant empire to managing the covert movement of arms and soldiers around the world. Some of the military leaders would not believe (at first) that a master chef could have so sharp a mind, would not believe she could turn from butter to guns, but she would not be denied. Later, when the Jagaren found the secret tactical bunker in Montana and killed most of our generals, she kept the Resistance from falling apart. Ever since, she's been leading most of the war efforts in North America.

I have no wartime talents. I'm a good cook, but nothing more. I was helpless to do anything to save myself or my friends when Dallas fell.

My friends are surely dead by now, tortured to death to amuse their captors. Everything seems to be for the Jagaren's amusement, even the war to take the planet. I have no doubt they could have used a biological weapon from the safety of their spaceships to wipe us all out. But that wouldn't have been any *fun* for them. They *like* seeing their slave troops clash in bloody, primitive conflict with our people. I suspect that the Jagaren are their world's spoiled, sadistic rich children who've been sent off to vent their twisted aggressions in war games well away from home. Or maybe they've come on their own, like the boys who used to wander my neighborhood in search of stray cats to set on fire, their apathetic parents oblivious to their misdeeds. I can't imagine how their civilization evolved if they're *all* like this.

I have not been physically abused much. They know I need my strength to cook for them. And they want to keep me alive because I am my mother's only child, and there is the chance she will try to rescue me.

Every day, I try to warn her away. I know she gets my messages. When I was very small, we learned that if one of us slept while the other was awake, the sleeper would dream of the other's activities. If we both slept at the same time, we shared the same dreams. My connection to her has weakened as I've grown older, but she's told me her connection to my mind has remained as strong as the day I was born. Almost all my dreams have followed her life, although I can't always see it clearly. She is my only window to the free world. I can only imagine that it is the same for her, that now she must dream of dismembering and cooking little boys.

I finish skinning the corpse. I set the skin aside for chopping and deep-frying, pick up the bone saw and survey his stripped flesh with my butcher's eye. He smells like raw lamb. His arms, ribs, and most of his legs will have to become barbecue. I pull a stout knife from the block and start to separate his joints. Very little of him can be made into steak, but I will try with his glutes and quadriceps. I have to try to meet the menu, or I will be punished, and my punishment will be my mother's nightmares.

I tried to commit suicide my very first day as the Jagaren's cook. Loudspeakers ordered me into the kitchen from my cell that first morning. I found seven babies lined up on the counter, with instructions to roast them like suckling pigs. I stared at the menu for a while, then got a knife and cut my own throat.

The Jagaren kept me from dying, of course. While my body healed, they walled my mind in a VR hell, piping in the recorded final memories of people they'd tortured to death. By all rights, the experience should have shattered my sanity, but my mother's stability saved me.

But I dare not try suicide again, for I cannot bear to inflict such nightmares on her. Furthermore, in my dreams she *orders* me to do their bidding, to do whatever I must to survive. That's always been our family's way. My ancestors survived every sort of war and atrocity. My great-great-grandmother, as a little girl, survived the massacres in Rwanda by hiding in a pile of corpses for three days. Two hundred years ago during WWII, one of my Jewish ancestors was put in the camps in Poland. They set him to work prying the gold out of the mouths of the people they gassed or shot. He survived, and afterward moved to the U.S. where he became a very successful dentist. Just to spite the Nazis, no doubt, because I'm sure he had no real desire to touch a tooth ever again. Even if he'd been a sadist, he'd have hated the work.

I wonder if I will be able to cook again, if I ever get out of here alive. I wonder if I will ever be able to hold a child or lover in my arms without my fingers automatically seeking the places a knife should be inserted to crack apart their joints.

The boy is completely dismembered now. I set his hands, arms, and shins on a rack for the barbecue. Then I slice open his abdomen to figure out what will be sausage, and what will be chitterlings.

I wonder if I and my mother are the first in our family to have shared minds, shared souls. It's hard to tell because we've kept our connection an utter and complete secret for fear that we'd be locked up for examination. No doubt any others would do the same. But such a thing has to be as much a matter of genes as it is a matter of spirit. How can a four-year-old girl find the courage to stay still and silent, without food or water, in the midst of stinking corpses for half a week? How can a young man be made to rob the corpses of his friends and neighbors for five years and survive sane and unbroken? Perhaps they, too, dreamed of freedom through a loved one's eyes.

I work hard and fast the rest of the day (if it is in fact day; all the clocks in here tell me how much time I *have*, not what time it *is*). I make the pie crust, chop the apples and tomatoes, stew the collards. The boy's large muscles are breaded and fried and covered in cream gravy, his limbs and ribs coal-smoked for hours and drowned in sweet barbecue sauce, stomach and large intestine chopped and stewed for chitterlings, skin chopped and deep fried into puffy rinds. The rest of him becomes sausage.

I never taste the meat dishes directly, only the sauces and the vegetable dishes. I have a good knowledge of spices and how they blend, so if I'm careful with my measurements I don't make mistakes.

Not that I really have any idea of how the Jagaren' sense of taste works. They aren't human, after all. Although they are warm-blooded, they don't resemble any Earth mammal in the least.

It took the Resistance some time to capture a Jagaren for study and vivisection. The Jagaren's slave troops are composed of species from many other worlds, including humans and even some Earth animals now that the Jagaren have had a few years to study the mammalian brain. All their slaves are turned into murderous automatons via viral reprogramming of their brains and are fitted with bioelectronic radio receivers in case their orders should change. No officers, just the soldiers in battle 'til they die while the Jagaren are well away from the fighting.

But the Resistance captured a tourist in the rubble of Boston: one of the Jagaren had apparently wanted to see a little blood and thunder up close. Mother, knowing full well the risk of telepathy, made sure it was kept in a dark, soundless chamber until they found an anesthetic that would keep it under.

I saw some of the inspections and vivisections through my mother's eyes. I suspect I may have appreciated the procedures more than she, since I studied biology in college. A squat creature it was, beautiful and hideous at the same time, its tentacled body covered in bright green and blue feathery scales. I wondered how they managed to capture it; the Jagaren was radially symmetrical, with an eye pointing out at each corner of its square skull. It's hard to sneak up on something with 360-degree vision. I guess they ran it down; the Jagaren's four stout legs were good for kicking and climbing, but too short for speed.

When they cut it open, the fleshy steam smelled like fish. The vivisection revealed an incredible digestive system: a multi-chambered stomach, with colonies of bacteria to break down cellulose, bone, even some types of rock. And it could probably eat just about anything; the mouth was a wide, sphincter-lipped cavity at the top of its head (the brain was set out of harm's way in the torso). The muscular oral cavity was lined with circular rows of grinding teeth, and in between were millions of taste buds. Far more than we poor mammals have, and far more specialized.

So even if I prepare everything to taste exactly as it should to humans, the Jagaren might hate it and punish me. Of course, they might like it, and punish me anyway.

When the meal is ready, I prepare the twelve dinner plates and dessert dishes and set them on the conveyor belt that carries the food away to be eaten. The conveyor belt door is maybe just barely big enough for me to try to squeeze through (I've lost a lot of weight since I've been here), but the thought of being in the Jagaren's dining hall is unspeakably terrifying. They would devour me, I'm sure, gourmands gobbling down a bit of sushi. To feel my arms and legs being sucked into those grinding maws, my bone and flesh shredding as surely as if my limbs had been thrust down a garbage disposal...no. I stay as far from the door as I can.

There is only one other way out of the kitchen: the door to the hallway that leads to my cell. Or *cells*, I should say. I go into the hallway, sit down on the concrete floor, and wait. There are three doors in front of me. The one on the right leads to a room with a soft hotel bed, a toilet, a shower, soap, and a change of clean clothes; I will get this room if the Jagaren enjoy their meal. Behind the middle door is a bare concrete room with a futon, sink and toilet; I get this if the meal is indifferent. If the meal is unsatisfactory, I get the last room, a cold, cramped, brightly-lit cell with nothing but a sink and toilet. The Jagaren do not want their cook to be contaminated with excrement.

I cannot simply spend the night in the hallway or the kitchen. Once, when I refused to respond to the loudspeakers, they sent knock-out gas through the vents. The corpse-movers carried me to the small cold cell. I woke with a headache that lasted three days.

I wait for one hour, two. Finally, the buzzer sounds, and the right door swings open. The Jagaren were pleased. I should sleep well tonight.

I enter the room, and find the concrete shard I've hidden beneath the bed. I pull off my shirt, and stare down at my scarred chest and belly. One cut for each man, woman, and child I've butchered for the Jagaren; almost every inch of my torso is engraved. I find a smooth place, right above my sternum. I push the sharp end of the shard into my flesh and slowly rake it down, again and again, until blood washes dark and soap-slick over my pale skin.

I dream of my mother. She is feverish. Lances of fire arc through her veins with every step she takes down the dark corridors of the bunker. Her generals take her to a briefing room, where they tell her of an island in the Caribbean. They have found where the Jagaren are holding me, and are going to stage a rescue mission.

My mother will go with them.

They are treating it as a suicide mission. I desperately want to tell her to stop. I'm not worth it; she is dying, yes, but her last days could surely be spent better than *this*. But I can be nothing more than a mute observer.

And all the while, my mother thinks: *300 degrees, 300 degrees, don't go over 300 degrees. You will know what to do.*

I wake up crying, bile in my throat. My mother is going to kill herself for me. She is everything to the fate of the human race, and she is going to *waste* herself, just because I am her child. Her helpless, useless child.

Soon, the morning alarm blares through the room, and the door slides open. The loudspeakers order me into the kitchen. It's always like this; the whole thing is automated.

In the kitchen, I find two young women and an order for French fare. The recipes are demanding, and I cannot concentrate on my work. I burn the bread and scorch the sauces, and at the end of the day I am sent to the tiny, cold concrete room where it is nearly impossible to sleep. I do not dream much, and that is a mercy.

I walk through my work a tear-stained zombie, half awake and half asleep. I feel as though I've been wrapped in an invisible shroud. Sound, light, touch, all my senses are muffled. My fingers are clumsy and numb. I spill more food on the floor than I get into the pots.

Just as I set the last of the poorly-cooked fajitas and enchiladas on the conveyor belt, a searing pain shoots through my thigh. Suddenly, my blood races with adrenaline. Gunfire and screams ring inside my head. A stabbing pain rips into my chest, and I pass out.

Later, I come to in my small cold cell. My heart is beating strongly, and I realize what I felt was my mother's death.

The human race is lost. I sit huddled with my head on my knees for a long time, unable to even cry. Finally, I drift off to a dreamless, black sleep.

The next morning, on the butcher block I find my mother and two young men with Marine Corps tattoos on their forearms. Stark against their pale skin are purpling, quarter-sized bullet holes. My mother has been shot through her right thigh and between her breasts.

My whole body is shaking, a tic in my eyelid making my vision twitch. But my mind is dead and cold. I can feel nothing, no rage, no grief, nothing. This is my waking nightmare, and everything I see and touch has taken on the distant, insubstantial sheen of dream.

Only my work is left; everything else is gone. I pull the paper from my mother's mouth. The Jagaren want an Ethiopian meal today. Dinner for sixty. This is twice the number I've ever had to serve before. Apparently, they've all come out to devour her.

I will have to work fast, and my mother's flesh will have to go a long way. I pick up my skinning knife and start to prepare the corpses. As I start to skin one Marine, I realize that his flesh looks strange. His fat is ever so slightly bluish, and his blood vessels are thickened. How can such a young, fit man have arteriosclerosis? I turn to my mother, and slice open her leg. She has the same blued fat, the same hardened vessels.

I dig deeper and cut open her femoral artery with my knife. Inside the plaque that is almost blocking the vessel I see the shine of minute blue crystals. If the plaque showed up on a CAT scan or MRI, it would simply look like advanced cardiovascular disease.

My mother's thoughts echo in my memory: *300 degrees, don't go above 300 degrees. You will know what to do.*

The realization hits me, and I curse myself for not catching on sooner, for letting my grief blind me to what my mother planned. Virus. The plaques contain crystallized clumps of virus, resistant to denaturing up to 300 degrees.

I stare at their exposed flesh. They're absolutely *loaded* with the virus. Suddenly, the cause of my mother's fevers and surgeries is clear to me—she's been letting the doctors turn her into a walking bioweapon.

I cut out some of their arteries and leave them to soak in a cauldron of warm water; I will use this to make the batter for the thin pancakes used to scoop up the food. The pancakes cook at about 200 degrees and, with luck, the artery-water will render them virulent. I take several pounds of fat from my mother and the Marines and pulverize it in the food processor until it's a fine paste. This will enrich the sauces and the lentil paste, after they have cooked and cooled down a bit.

I work constantly, sweating from the heat of the kitchen and my own anticipation. The cut over my heart breaks open, staining the front of my shirt with blood.

I get the banquet prepared barely in time. It's beautiful; I haven't done this well in weeks. There's enough food for half of them to have seconds.

As I set the plates on the conveyor belt, I say grace.

"We thank thee, Lord, for these Thy gifts which they are about to receive from Thy bounty and through Christ, our Lord, amen."

My mother is standing beside me. She squeezes my shoulder gently.

"It's a very good dinner, dear," she tells me. "I wouldn't have put quite so much pepper in the lentils, but a very good dinner just the same."

"Thanks, Mom." I pause, not knowing how to express how terribly sorry I am for what I've just done to her. When I look over, I realize she's not really there. She'll never be there again.

After the wait in the hallway, I am sent to the best room. I cut myself for a while, carving a cross into my chest, then take a long, hot shower and lie down. I'm still shaking, my heart pounding. Will it work? What will they do to me if it doesn't?

Whatever happens, this is the end of my career as a cook.

I lie awake, mind churning. I've cooked my own mother. Sliced her, and diced her, and made her into a beautiful gravy-covered communion for our new lords. Will I be freed, when so many better people have suffered and died? Or will I join them in a horrible death? Which fate do I really prefer?

And I can't stand this God-damned *waiting*! If I am to die, then I want to *die* already! If I am to live, then I want *out*!

My thoughts wind me so tight I can't stay still. I get up, pace, babble nonsense rhymes to myself, anything to drown out the roar in the back of my head.

When the timed alarm finally sounds and the door opens, I race into the kitchen, my skin prickling with manic fear.

The carving block is bare. I have no corpse, no instructions. The refrigerator hasn't been re-stocked.

"What!" I scream at the loudspeakers. "No meat? How can I make your pudding when you won't leave me any meat!"

I run to the conveyor belt and peer down the ten-foot-long shaft. I see dim light, but no movement.

"Allee allee out's in free!" I call.

No response, no sound. The thought of crawling through this thing to the dining room is unspeakably terrifying. But what's terror worth when you've cooked your mommy?

I climb onto the conveyor belt. Sensing my weight, the motor starts automatically and slowly carries me into the shaft. The heat lamps lining the ceiling come on, filling the shaft with red-orange light. Almost instantly, the shaft is sweltering. The light burns into my back, my scalp, my face. Sweat pours off me, and my itchy cuts start leaking blood again. I'm stewing in my own skin. It suddenly occurs to me that I should be on a platter with a nice side of cranberry sauce. The thought makes me giggle, and for a long time I can't stop.

An eternity later, I come out of the shaft into the huge, airy dining room. The breeze hitting my roasted face is wonderfully cool and feels like the breath of God.

The room is filled with rows and rows of long wooden tables without chairs. There are a few dirty plates still scattered on the tables. The place is dead quiet, abandoned. Dull light from the overcast sky filters through high bay windows. Even this weak radiance makes me squint like a newborn baby; it's been years since I've seen the sun.

"Hey! Come and eat me, already!" My voice echoes hollowly.

I turn around, and see a set of double doors. One is ajar, swinging gently in the breeze. I jump off the conveyor belt and run to the door, my arms raised as if I am a dove about to take flight. I push out into the warm Caribbean air. I smell the ocean, and flowers.

And something rotting. I nearly trip over a Jagaren that lies just outside the door. I squat and stare at the corpse. The stout body is covered with deep, oozing ulcers, and the ground is littered with its molt of feathery scales. The flies have found it, and are bustling for a sip of ichor and a chance to lay eggs in the fishy flesh. The maggots will have quite a feast.

I leave the corpse and walk down the path to a gazebo that overlooks the ocean. The sun is a red orb just above the horizon, lighting the streaked clouds with delicate purples and pinks. I don't know whether it's rising or setting.

In the distance, I hear helicopters.

Cthylla

An urn in the lovely Chapel of the Chimes bears the epitaph "Natalya Moroz, Artist and Muse and Misguided Soul." An incomplete summation of a life that burned short and very bright. But the label does not tell anything close to the whole story of the ashes in this lovely work of ceramic and paint. For that, we need to take a closer look at a young woman named Kamerynne Craigie, whose story we know from diary entries, recovered texts and email....

When she was 8, Kamerynne Craigie heard a joke at school: "Did you hear about the British rock star who married the supermodel? Their baby had his looks and her talent!"

It wasn't the kind of joke that 8-year-olds think up; some kid heard it from a comic on cable TV. But there, in their Silicon Valley private school, the joke seemed edgy and grown-up and so the boy brayed it out at lunch and everybody laughed, even some of the kids whose parents actually were musicians with model wives. Kamerynne laughed, too, halfheartedly, not really understanding it until another boy told her, "It's cuz the Rolling Stones all had kids that are really ugly and they can't play guitar."

But something about it didn't sit right. Afterward her mind held onto the joke, turning it over and over like a Rubik's cube she couldn't solve more than one side of.

When she was thirteen, her Aunt Cherity died. The Saturday after the funeral, Kamerynne was in the shower and finally realized: *The joke is about me. I'm that joke.*

The revelation was so profound that she stumbled back against the tile wall, slid down into the tub and blinked numbly while the water droplets slapped against her face.

I'm that joke.

Her father, Cameron Craigie, was a computer genius. He'd dropped out in his freshman year at Cal Tech to start up a software company in a friend's garage, back when that was a legitimate career move for whiz kids. Kamerynne had his frizzy brown hair and chubby cheeks, and she made As and Bs in school, just as he had, but nobody had ever suggested that genius was a thing she was capable of.

Her mother Grayce wasn't a genius, but she was beautiful and talented and everyone loved her. She'd even been nominated for an Oscar for her role as the lead in an indie film called *Cthylla*, but she didn't win. Her father met Grayce at the movie's Sundance party, nine months before Kamerynne was born. As far as Kamerynne knew, they hadn't shared a bed since then, but they both grew up in old-fashioned households and they believed in the institution of marriage, particularly when a child was involved. Past that, neither of them carried any particular expectations into the marriage, and they were able to coexist pleasantly as roommates in his Mill Valley ranch house.

Her father seemed content with Kamerynne—"Let a kid be a kid," he'd always say—but as the years went on her mother bore a palpable air of disappointment. Kamerynne tried singing and school plays but she had a hard time remembering lyrics and lines and standing up in front of a bunch of strangers inevitably tied her tongue. Nobody seemed eager for her to get up on stage anyhow, not with her unfashionable pudge and poofy hair.

When Kamerynne was very young, her mother used to call her "my little changeling" and it wasn't until the girl read a book of fairy tales that it dawned on her that the term had nothing to do with diapers. After the Oscar nomination, her mother got a lot of acting offers. She wasn't ever the leading lady, but she was often her best friend or a quirky neighbor. So Grayce Aberdine (she kept her maiden name) always had a shoot someplace, or an appointment with her shrink or her acting coach, or she was off at a spiritual retreat.

I'm that joke, Kamerynne thought again. She'd looked up a picture of Keith Richards' son Marlon once at the school library. He wasn't bad-looking, she thought, certainly not *ugly* like the girl next to her declared he was, and she figured he was surely better at guitars than she'd ever be at acting or coding. But whatever pretty good thing he did wasn't good enough for the world when you had famous, brilliant parents.

Kamerynne sometimes wondered if she'd just been prettier, more like an actress, if things would have been different. She wondered if her mother would have found reasons to be home instead of off worshipping some goddess at the beach or centering her chakras. But on the other hand a lot of the kids complained about their moms getting up in their business all the time. The housekeepers who watched Kamerynne mostly let her do what she wanted as long as she got her homework done and finished the book lists her father left for her (he didn't think the school focused enough on reading). Her dad was gone a lot, too, but he had his company to run. Years later, Kamerynne would come to realize that his absence was just as much a choice as her mother's, but when she was 13 her mother's behavior seemed simultaneously more deliberate and more erratic.

Her mother's sister Cherity stepped in to fill the unspoken maternal void when Kamerynne was three. Where her mom was willowy and elegant, Cherity was stocky and strong. Her aunt played softball for a team called the Oakland Outlanders, and Kamerynne loved going to games. She and her aunt had the same way of smiling and laughing and they both really loved *The Muppet Show*. Once, when they were hiking in Redwood Park, someone mistook them for mother and daughter, and Kamerynne was secretly pleased.

But then her aunt started feeling too ill to play ball or go hiking, and she went to the doctor and found out she had blood cancer. She still took Kamerynne out places, not as often because the chemo really took it out of her, but everyone spoke of it as just a temporary thing. Kamerynne's father had money for the most talented doctors and he promised that Cherity would get the very best care.

Almost exactly two years after her diagnosis, Cherity died.

As the water beat down on her, Kamerynne had her second epiphany of the morning: *I'm going to die, too.*

She felt her mortality through and through, and it was abjectly terrifying. Her body would turn into something like that steak her mom had forgotten in the trunk of the Jaguar for a week, stinking and slimy and crawling with maggots. She'd cease to exist. Would her soul go to heaven? What if there *wasn't* a heaven? What if *this*—this frustrating, confusing, unasked-for existence on Earth—was all she'd have?

Her parents had their fame. People wrote her mom fan mail and, because *Cthylla* had become a cult favorite, some people had tattooed her character's face on their bodies. Nobody used her father's face for a tattoo, but his picture had been on the cover of *Time.* His software ran computers that ran hospitals that kept people alive. They were both heroes. They'd be *remembered.*

What about her? Her teachers and her mother and father spoke of everyone having an individual calling, a place in the world. But what if that wasn't true? What if she was only ever going to be pretty good at things that didn't really matter, and there wasn't a place for her soul to go afterward? Was there a reason she was here on Earth, other than that one night her mother and her father both went to a party, got a little tipsy and didn't bother with condoms?

What if her life was just a meaningless accident?

It was suddenly hard to breathe. Inside her, it felt as though an enormous, cold, unfathomable blackness had opened up, and she was teetering, about to fall into it. She wanted to run screaming down the street, as though she could outrun death and the pain of mediocrity. But some kid at school had run naked down the street once and lurking paparazzi took pictures and his whole family was embarrassed. The kid had to see a shrink and surrender his thoughts and feelings every week like one of the kids in *Oliver Twist* giving his money to Fagin.

Kamerynne didn't want to see a shrink. She was afraid that talking about her fears out loud might make them real, like saying "Bloody Mary" three times in front of a mirror. So she stood up on unsteady legs, turned off the water, got dressed, and went into her bedroom to play *Kirby's Adventure* for the rest of the day.

Three years passed in which Kamerynne went to school, didn't cultivate any friends, and played video games and read thick fantasy novels (when she wasn't reading one of her father's endless book assignments) to keep herself from thinking about death and the probable meaninglessness of her existence. She wasn't getting into drugs or drinking like some of her classmates, so her parents mostly just vaguely fretted about her lack of fresh air and exercise and made the housekeeper take her to the gym three times a week. Her mother sometimes spoke of getting her some liposuction and plastic surgery when she was ready for college. Her father started sitting with her to show her how to code, and he took her to work with him more often, showing her bits and pieces of his business. She was being tested, she could tell, and although she tried to please him, she couldn't work up much enthusiasm. And he seemed to sense that.

"You like games, right? You could become a game designer," he said as they got ice cream at the company cafe. "It would be harder, because you're a girl, but you could do it."

"I could." She swirled the hot fudge into her sundae with her spoon, not sure if he meant it would be harder because girls just weren't very good at designing games or it would be harder because people would be dismissive if she tried. "But would it matter?"

He frowned, puzzled. "Matter? What do you mean?"

She realized she'd said the first "Bloody Mary" and quickly shrugged, blushing. "I don't know."

Kamerynne might have spent the rest of her teen years and young adulthood in a video game cocoon if her mother hadn't caught Darla, their housekeeper, smoking a joint by the pool. Her mother fired Darla and three days later brought in a new woman named Olga Moroz who was very pretty; her mother said she'd been an actress back in the Ukraine and they'd met at a spiritual retreat. Olga went about her chores with quick, silent efficiency. After Kamerynne tried to make small talk, she realized the woman couldn't speak much English, which was probably why she hadn't been able to get many acting jobs in the U.S.

On the third weekend of Olga's tenure as their new housekeeper, she brought a teenaged girl with her.

"Is my daughter, Natalya," Olga explained. "I hope you do not mind."

"It's fine," Kamerynne replied, her throat suddenly dry. Natalya was like nobody she'd ever seen before. Certainly she'd seen the individual parts of Natalya's wardrobe on a hundred other girls: the magenta-and-black bob, the silver nose ring, the black jeans and Doc Martens and Bauhaus tee shirt. But it wasn't her wardrobe, or her porcelain skin, or her dark green eyes. There was something *luminous* about the girl, something beyond mere physical beauty that Kamerynne would never have the words to describe.

Natalya never noticed Kamerynne gawking at her because her own eyes were fixed on the huge painting of the *Cthylla* movie poster on the living room wall.

"Oh. My. God! That is my *favorite* movie!" Natalya gushed. She stepped forward and touched the polished mahogany frame reverently. "Grayce Aberdine was *amazing* as the priestess. She should have won an Oscar. She was *robbed.*"

"She's my mom," Kamerynne said, trying to sound cool. "This is her house."

"What!" Natalya looked shocked and did a little dance as if she was trying to levitate, afraid to have her mere-mortal feet touching the creamy white carpet of her movie idol. Then she danced around to face her mother. "Mom…?"

"Is true!" Her mother beamed, clearly aware that she'd just earned herself premium Cool Mom points.

Natalya let out a delighted shriek and practically bowled Olga over giving her a bear hug. "You are the best! Ohmigod this is the best!"

"Loves you, too. But work. I have to." Her mother gently pushed her away.

"Hey, um, Natalya." Kamerynne had fallen out of the habit of trying to impress anyone, but now every neuron in her brain was firing, fixed on solving the problem of making this amazing luminous girl like her.

"Nat. My friends call me Nat." She pushed her magenta bangs out of her eyes.

"We could go watch the director's extended cut of *Cthylla* downstairs in the theatre if you want."

Nat frowned and squinted as though she suspected Kamerynne of playing a prank. "What? There's no director's cut."

"Oh yeah there is. It just isn't out yet; they haven't even told the trade mags because the director is still messing with it. He had to cut some scenes to get it down to an R—"

Nat clapped her hands and pogoed excitedly. "Omigod yes!"

Kamerynne led her down the big spiral staircase to the theatre that her mother always called a screening room. It seated twenty-four people in three rows lined with little blue LEDs along the aisles. The screen was a genuine antique her parents had rescued from an old theatre before it was torn down. Her mother said it was the first place she'd ever seen a movie.

"If you want, there's soda and candy and stuff." Kamerynne waved toward the wet bar at the back of the room.

"You got any Sprite and vodka?"

"Um...yeah." Kamerynne felt a pang of guilt; her mother was into clean living and would not approve. But she felt far too anxious to tell Nat "no."

So she just turned on the media server and queued up the movie while Nat made herself a tall drink. They settled down on the front row, the screen huge above them, and Kamerynne hit "play" on the remote.

Kamerynne hadn't actually seen more than bits and pieces of her mother's movie—her parents said it wasn't suitable for children. She wasn't a child anymore, but she hadn't gotten around to watching it, either. It seemed like old news somehow. She'd heard everyone chat about it so much that she'd *felt* as though she'd seen it about twenty times over.

But the talk and the trailers hadn't truly prepared her for the film, and as the opening credits rolled, she found herself mesmerized by the dark, strange story about a cult of women raising an ancient goddess from the ocean. The goddess was like a mermaid, if the bottom half of a mermaid was an octopus instead of a fish. She wondered if the animators at Disney had seen the movie and ripped off the goddess to create Ursula the Sea Witch in *The Little Mermaid*. But Ursula was all cartoon wickedness and the goddess in *Cthylla* was terrifying and breathtaking.

"It's all real, you know," Nat whispered as the eight-legged goddess rose from the water flickering above them.

"What?" Kamerynne blinked at her, feeling disoriented; she'd gotten so engrossed in the movie she'd nearly forgotten Nat was there.

"Well, it's not real now, but it *will* be, someday."

"Oh." Kamerynne blinked again, suspecting she'd missed something important, and then she realized that Nat's hand was on her knee. Suddenly she felt as though her stomach was filled with a hundred buzzing, stingless bees.

"This is so hot," Nat breathed, staring raptly at the screen.

Kamerynne looked up again, and her mother had dropped her red priestess robe and was standing there completely bare-ass naked, embracing the glistening goddess, whose purple tentacles were creeping up her bare legs....

"Jesus. That's my *mom*. I can't watch this." Kamerynne could feel herself blushing right down to the soles of her feet.

She began to stand, but Nat grabbed her wrist.

"Don't go," she said. "Just sit on my lap and look at me instead."

Nat was pulling her wrist insistently, not letting go, so Kamerynne knelt across the girl's slender legs and blinked at her as she gazed at the screen over her shoulder. Kamerynne tried to ignore the moans and wet noises coming in crisp remastered Dolby audio through the speakers. Nat held both of Kamerynne's hands very tightly, her breath perfumed with alcohol.

"When I first saw you, I didn't think you looked anything at all like your mom," Nat whispered, not taking her eyes off whatever was happening on the screen behind Kamerynne. "But now I can see it. You have her neck and her ears."

And suddenly, Nat was kissing her just below her left ear, and Kamerynne's body filled with decalescent electricity, and she no longer gave a damn about what the cephalopod goddess was doing to her mother in the movie.

A month later, the two girls sat making out on Kamerynne's bed.

"Could I, like, show you something?" Nat asked, oddly shy.

Kamerynne had seen Nat top to bottom, so what could possibly make her this bashful? "Sure, anything."

"Okay, but I mean, don't laugh if you think it's stupid or whatever."

"I'm not gonna think it's stupid. Just show me."

"'Kay." Nat retrieved her black nylon Jansport backpack from the floor, unzipped it and pulled out a sketchbook. "I sorta want to be an artist someday, and I just sort of wanted you to see my stuff...."

Kamerynne opened the sketchbook, and at first she thought she was looking at a black-and-white photograph of a man with rats' toothed maws where his eyes should have been, but then she saw the smudge of pencil graphite and realized it was a hyperrealistic sketch. She carefully turned the page, and saw another: this was a woman in a tawdry hotel room cradling a baby made entirely of insects' eyes. The book contained page after page of beautiful monstrosity.

"You did all these?" Kamerynne asked.

"Yeah, I mean, they're not how I want them to be, but maybe someday...."

"What do you mean 'someday'? These are amazing, right now! These are, like, better than the art that my dad drops a grand on down at the galleries!"

"Aw, you're a sweetheart. But nah, I'm not that good."

"I mean, okay, I'm not an expert, but my dad made me read like fifty billion art books. This is really *really* good. I mean, you *are* an artist, right now. Why do you think it's not good?"

"I just...I just want to get what's in my head down on paper, you know? I want it to look the same as I see it in my mind, but it never does. It never comes *close*. I'm okay with pencils, I guess, but I need to get better with oil and acrylic. Maybe I need to learn how to work a computer or whatever."

"So learn to work a computer." Kamerynne blinked at her.

"I don't have the money to buy a computer, and I feel weird working on my stuff at the computers at the library. People see naked bits and freak out. And the library doesn't even have Photoshop or anything I could really use anyway."

In that moment, Kamerynne experience another major revelation: she herself might have no talents to speak of, but Nat had a talent that absolutely took her breath away. And it would be so easy to help her become the artist she was clearly born to be. Maybe helping was Kamerynne's reason for being alive on the Earth.

"Put your shirt back on; I'm taking you to the mall. You want a laptop or a desktop?"

Nat stared at her as if she'd sprouted a tentacle in the middle of her forehead. "Are you serious?"

"Totally. Let's go."

A year later, Kamerynne was sticking her finger down Nat's throat in a filthy McDonald's restroom in Oakland, desperately trying to get her to throw up the bottle of tranquilizers she'd swallowed. It seemed obvious to Kamerynne, finally, that someone like Nat who had such wild nightmares spilling out of her imagination might have had some of that darkness seep into and poison her soul. And truly helping her might be a bit more harrowing than spending a few dollars here and there.

"Why'd you do that?" Kamerynne asked, wondering whether she wanted to cry or slap Nat as the other girl retched melting blue pills and orange juice and vodka into the stained toilet. "You're my best friend; you could have talked to me."

Nat collapsed back on the piss-stained floor, shaking her head. "Nah. You'd be berr off wi'out me."

"I love you."

"I hate me," she sobbed.

Kamerynne picked up Nat after she was released from the hospital.

"I have to go to the pharmacy to get some meds." She smoothed the crumpled prescription on her lap.

"Okay. Matter which one?" Kamerynne turned the key in her BMW's ignition.

"Nope."

They drove in silence for a few minutes.

"I'm sorry I scared you," Nat said.

"It's okay," Kamerynne replied. "It could have been a lot worse." She cleared her throat. "You know, I wouldn't be better off without you. I love you."

"I love you too," Nat said.

"I *forbid* you from dying, okay?"

Nat laughed. "It doesn't work that way, I don't think."

"You're smart, you're beautiful, and you're so much more talented than anybody I've ever met...look, if you decide *you* don't deserve to live, how are the rest of us supposed to feel like we deserve to keep breathing, huh?" Kamerynne meant for it to all sound like a joke, but when the words left her mouth, she realized it wasn't the least bit funny.

Nat smiled at her anyhow. "It's different for you. I see the Goddess in my dreams, and I know I'm a disappointment to her."

Kamerynne swallowed. Nat mentioned the Goddess sometimes, just in passing, but when Kamerynne asked her about her religion, Nat always said she wasn't really supposed to talk about it. The whole thing seemed weird, but she didn't want to be disrespectful. "How could you disappoint her?"

"I have a role in her Coming. Not now, but later. And I'm too scared to do it. I'm a coward, and I'm worthless, and She knows it."

"Hey, no, you're not worthless; don't talk about yourself like that, okay?"

"I am." Nat began to weep.

Kamerynne squeezed the steering wheel, feeling lost and helpless, but then she remembered the pills they were driving to get. The meds would surely help clear Nat's mind. Kamerynne vowed to make sure she took her meds on time and stayed away from alcohol.

Kamerynne's mother swept into the house with an enormous smile on her face.

"Oh, darling, you're here! I have the most wonderful news!"

"What's up, Mom?"

"Charibdys Studios has gotten the funding for *Cthylla: The Rising*! They want me to reprise my role."

"Oh, wow, that's great!" Part of Kamerynne cringed as she remembered the tentacled screen embrace.

"I've talked to your father, and he's interested in being a producer this time around, so we're meeting with the studio president and some of his execs aboard his yacht this evening. We should be home by 11:00, I think."

Shortly after midnight, Kamerynne got a call from the police. A propane tank exploded onboard the yacht, and the force knocked her parents off the deck. Unconscious and helpless, they drowned. They were dead.

The next morning, she found that *Cthylla* fans had left a massive pile of roses and lilies outside the front gate.

Kamerynne met with her parents' lawyer after the funeral.

"It seems your parents made some changes to their will that I was unaware of and would have advised against," he said gravely. "But nonetheless the alterations are legitimate and legal."

"What changes?" she asked. She'd had a hard time feeling anything but numb since the phone call. Her parents' bodies were too badly damaged for an open casket funeral, and so their deaths still felt unreal.

"Your father and mother have both left 80% and 90%, respectively, of their money to the Messina Strait Foundation."

"What's that?"

"It's a religious organization, one that your mother was apparently involved with most of her adult life. According to the notarized letter she left behind, she apparently joined it either before or during her work on *Cthylla*, and your father became involved recently. It's news to me, too," he added, apparently reading the confusion on her face.

"What does the foundation do?"

"They offer spiritual retreats and workshops. Past that, I'm honestly not sure, except that now they have a great deal of money with which to do it."

Kamerynne couldn't help Nat or anyone else without money. And if she couldn't help...what good was she?

"Am I broke?" She immediately hated how much her question made her sound like a little girl.

"Oh, no, don't worry...you still have your parents' house, and they left you a trust fund that should enable you to maintain the house and pay for your college and personal upkeep indefinitely. You should be able to live comfortably without having to work unless you want to."

"I do want to work," she said. "I want to be...worthwhile."

She and Nat both started their freshman years at UCLA the next year. They left Olga to take care of her parents' house and they split a dorm room on campus. Nat majored in art, of course, and Kamerynne tentatively settled on journalism; she wasn't sure she wanted to try coding games, but writing about them for magazines seemed fun. And if she majored in English she knew she'd have to write a bunch of papers on a bunch of old books that had bored her half to death the first time her father made her read them.

The week before midterms, two events changed Kamerynne's life forever.

The first was that she attended a guest lecture offered by a visiting investigative journalist from *The New York Times*.

"There's *always* a paper trail," the journalist told them. "Every thought that every person physically writes down or sends through an email is recorded somewhere. Every communication leaves a ghost behind. If you jot down a note on a piece of paper resting on a phone book, and then you tear up that paper, guess what? The imprint of your pen marks are on the cover of the phone book. A good investigator can find that and read that. If you send an email, even if you and your recipient delete it? That message has traveled through a dozen routers, and that email can be packet sniffed or recorded. There's *always* a paper trail, even if it isn't paper."

Kamerynne sat up straighter in her seat. Bloody Mary didn't have to be spoken aloud anymore to summon her spectre, it seemed.

She was still mulling over palimpsests and packet sniffers when she arrived back at their dorm room. "Paint it Black" was blasting on the stereo, and Nat was unconscious on the floor, barely breathing in a puddle of pill-spotted vomit.

Kamerynne spent five long hours by Nat's side at the ER. Nat regained consciousness briefly and started wailing and trying to pull out her nasogastric tube and IV. The doctors had to sedate her and told Kamerynne it was best if she went home.

So she went back to the dorm room; the janitorial staff had cleaned up the vomit in her absence, but the air in the room had a sour chemical smell. Kamerynne sat on her narrow bed and wept out her frustration and worry. Nat had seemed to be doing so well; she'd seemed *happy*. And her art had gotten even better! A gallery in LA was interested in showing her work. But clearly she wasn't actually happy...or something bad had happened.

Kamerynne booted up Nat's computer, composed a short, polite letter to let Nat's instructors know that she was in the hospital, and got into her email to start sending out messages.

In Nat's inbox was a message from someone named Dr. Helene Arcanjo:

Natalya,

It's very nice that the gallery is interested in your drawings, but remember that you must not focus on such trivial things. The Goddess has her plan for you, and you must dedicate yourself to her fully. Do not disappoint us after everything we've done for you.

-Helene

Who the hell was this Arcanjo woman? And what had she been doing for Nat? If Nat had confided in Arcanjo about her earlier suicide attempt, this email was as good as handing Nat a loaded pistol. A quick Web search revealed that Arcanjo had a PhD in divinity from the Innsmouth Theological Seminary in Rhode Island

and she was the minister for the Temple of the Deep Mother in Oxnard. As far as Kamerynne knew, Nat had never been to the church...but she couldn't be sure.

Not knowing made her sick to her stomach. What was going on in Nat's life? Kamerynne dug through Nat's email, looking for messages to or from Arcanjo. And there was nothing, no messages from other church members, not even any messages referring to the Goddess. If she was deleting the emails, Nat had to believe they contained something incriminating...and that there was a risk of someone looking for them.

Suddenly worried about leaving a search engine history on Nat's computer, Kamerynne went to her own computer. Another query on Temple of the Deep Mother led to an older version of the church page in archive.org that contained a list of members. Searches on those names led her to a church member's personal website, which contained a lot of poetry about the Goddess and links to several *Cthylla* fan pages, a couple of which mentioned Charybdis Studios. Whose representatives Kamerynne's mother and father had been meeting with the night they died.

The next morning, Kamerynne made some phone calls to former associates of her father's. When she told them what she wanted to know, most of them claimed ignorance or blew her off. Finally, she got in touch with a senior programmer who offered to call her back on another line. He gave her a name, and a campus address.

Kamerynne walked to Boelter Hall and found a small, windowless office on the third floor. The door was open a crack. Inside were two pale computer science students huddled around a Sun Microsystems computer. Their desks were piled high with diskettes, computer cables, and empty Mountain Dew cans.

She rapped on the door frame to get their attention. "Hi, is Chad Barnes in here?"

"Can we help you?" one of them asked, barely looking away from the code on the monitor.

"I hope so. My name's Kamerynne Craigie, and—"

"Are you Cameron Craigie's daughter?" His eyes focused on her like lasers.

Nat had the same star-struck expression when she found out she was standing in Grayce Aberdine's house.

"I am, in fact." She smiled at them, and suddenly they were both on their feet, talking over each other.

"Wow, it's an honor—"

"I was so bummed to hear about your dad, it was terrible—"

"I was hoping one of you guys could help me with a project," she said.

"Sure, what?" the first asked.

"I need everything you can tell me about keyloggers...."

Kamerynne disappeared into the computer science underworld at her college. She emerged long enough each day to visit Nat at the hospital, but beyond that she was in the computer lab learning what she could from Chad and his friends or at her own machine. She burrowed into cracking like a larvae in a juicy apple. The search for illicit knowledge and cryptic information excited her almost more than sex.

The day before Nat was released from the hospital, Kamerynne went to her computer to install a program to record keystrokes and copy her incoming email in a separate, hidden file on her hard drive. But as she dug into the computer's core system to install the hypervisor...she discovered another keylogger already running. It didn't look like any of the standard malware Chad had showed her. Kamerynne was able to decrypt enough of it to see that it was sending the data to a computer in the Ukraine. Nat's native country.

Kamerynne looked up the IP of the receiving computer, not expecting to find anything...but the address was registered to the European branch of Charybdis Studios.

A week after she picked up Nat from the hospital, Kamerynne downloaded a torrent of *Cthylla: The Rising*, which was still three months away from opening in theatres. She'd figured they'd gotten another actress to play her mother's role... but her mother's character wasn't in this film. She hadn't been recast; as far as this movie's script was concerned, her character had simply never existed. Had she been written out after her death? Or was she never supposed to be in the film in the first place?

Kamerynne took a screen capture of the list of supporters in the movie's end credits and spent several hours looking up names. Ten attended the Temple of the

Deep Mother at some point in their lives. And three seemed to have something to do with the Messina Strait Foundation, the group that had inherited her parents' money.

"What do you know about Charybdis Studios?" Kamerynne asked when Nat stumbled into their dorm room at three in the morning.

Nat paused in the doorway, her face flushed with alcohol. "A little. Not much. They made the *Cthylla* movies."

"Right." Kamerynne paused, not sure if she should continue. "Why would someone from those studios be monitoring your computer?"

Nat laughed dismissively, but also turned pale. "That's silly. That wouldn't happen."

"But it did." Kamerynne nodded toward her computer. "They're watching you. Why?"

Something seemed to crumple behind Nat's eyes, and she got a faraway expression. "To make sure I'm doing as I'm told."

Kamerynne's heart beat faster. Was she going to get the truth, at last? "What are they telling you to do?"

Tears spilled down Nat's cheeks. "Right now? Helene *wants* me help get rich people to donate to the Foundation. But I'm shit at it. Eventually I'm to go in the water, and the goddess will come out. She needs sacrifices to bring her into the world. It's what I was made for."

"Made for? What do you mean?"

Nat gave a shuddering little laugh. "It's funny, you know? You and I were both conceived at parties. Only your parents didn't mean to make you. Mine did. My mom had sex with every man at the temple so nobody would know who my father was. Thirteen guys, and she didn't get pregnant the first time, so they had to do it again during the next new moon. Me and all the other temple babies, we're goddess chum."

Kamerynne tried to get her mind around what Nat was telling her. "You're... you're saying you're supposed to be a human sacrifice?"

"Pretty much, yeah." Nat's face was a sickly grey.

"Why...why do they let you walk around? Go to college?"

"They don't care how I live my life; they just care that I'm there when it needs to end. And who knows when that will be? It could be next week, it could be in twenty years. And if it's in twenty years, I might as well be useful in the meantime, right?"

"Why don't you run away? Look, I'll give you money to run away."

Nat laughed again. She looked like she was going to start weeping at any moment. "There's no place to run. The Foundation is everywhere."

"The Messina Strait Foundation?"

"Yeah."

"How is the Foundation connected to the Temple of the Deep Mother and Charybdis Studios?"

"Isn't it obvious? The Foundation runs the studios and the Temple runs the Foundation."

Kamerynne stared at her for a moment, feeling herself dangling above that terrible, cold, unfathomable blackness she'd feared since she was a kid. "Did the Foundation kill my parents?"

"Probably, yeah. I mean, I don't know anything specific, but yeah. Once a wealthy person changes their will for the Foundation, they don't last long."

"Jesus. Fucking. Christ." Kamerynne wanted to scream. She wanted to cry. She wanted to push Nat's face right through the wall. "How can you be so casual about that? They murdered my parents! Does that not mean *anything* to you?"

"It's terrible! I agree! But...they do it every day."

Part of Kamerynne's mind was whispering *This can't be real* over and over. The room seemed to be tilted, the air a suffocating blanket. She looked down at her hands; they felt like they belonged to someone else.

"Why are you telling me all this?" Kamerynne's tongue felt like borrowed flesh, too, and was hard to move.

"Because it doesn't matter if you know or not. They won't kill me for telling, because they need me for the ritual. And they probably won't kill you, not unless you go to the papers or the cops or something stupid...and you're not stupid. They already have your money. And when the Goddess rises, everybody dies and none of this mattered. That's just how it goes."

A month later, Nat and a group of 100 other young women attended a beachside retreat near Bolinas, California. Helene Arcanjo led them into the water at high tide during a freak storm; all of them drowned. A pair of fishermen found Nat's body washed up on a nearby beach three days later.

Just hours after that, Kamerynne's BMW was found crashed and burned in a ravine; the body inside was so badly damaged it could not be conclusively identified.

Nat's cremains were interred in the lovely Chapel of the Chimes, courtesy of an anonymous donor.

Bank accounts and mutual funds belonging to the Messina Strait Foundation and Charybdis Studios developed mysterious electronic leaks, and in the space of a few months their assets plummeted so far that they had to seek bankruptcy protection. And after that, high-ranking members of the Foundation started turning up dead: a few car accidents, an electrocution in a bathtub, a heart attack in a hot tub, a plane crash.

Some people in the hacker community speculated that Kamerynne faked her death, re-emerging as a formidable grey hat named BldyM@ry, bent on destroying the Foundation and groups like it at all costs. Others claimed she was simply a dilettante who died of grief.

Regardless, the Goddess never rose from the depths.

But perhaps that's just a matter of time....

While the Black Stars Burn

Caroline tucked an unruly strand of coarse brown hair up under her pink knit cap, shrugged the strap of her black violin case back into place over her shoulder, and hurried up the music building stairs. Her skin felt both uncomfortably greasy and itched dryly under her heavy winter clothes; it had been seven days since the water heater broke in her tiny efficiency and the landlord wasn't answering his phone. Quick, chilly rag-baths were all she could stand, and she felt so self-conscious about the state of her hair that she kept it hidden under a hat whenever possible. She hoped that her violin professor Dr. Harroe wouldn't make her take her cap off.

Her foot slipped on a spot of dried salt on the stairs and she grabbed the chilly brass banister with her left hand to keep from pitching forward. The sharp, cold jolt made the puckered scar in her palm sharply ache, and the old memory returned fast and unbidden:

"Why aren't you practicing as I told you to?"

Her father scowled down at her. He was still in his orchestra conducting clothes: a grey blazer and black turtleneck. His fingers clenched a tumbler of Scotch over ice.

"M-my hand started to hurt." She shrank back against the hallway wall, hoping that she hadn't sounded whiny, hoping her explanation would suffice and he'd just send her to bed.

The smell of alcohol and sweat fogged the air around him, and that meant almost anything could happen. He wasn't always cruel. Not even usually. But talking to him when he'd been drinking was like putting a penny in a machine that sometimes dispensed glossy gumballs but other times a dozen stinging arachnids would swarm from the chute instead. And there was no way to know which she'd get, sweets or scorpions.

"Hurt?" he thundered down at her. "Nonsense! I'll show you what hurts!"

He grabbed her arm and dragged her to the fireplace in the music room. She tried to pull away, pleading, promising to practice all night if he wanted her to. But he was completely impassive as he drew a long dark poker from the rack and shoved it into the hottest part of the fire. He frowned down at the iron as the flames licked the shaft, seemingly deaf to her frantic mantra of *Please, no, Papa, I'll be good I swear please.*

The iron heated quickly, and in a series of motions as artful as any he'd performed on the orchestral podium he pulled it from the fire with one hand, squeezed her forearm hard to force her fingers open with the other, and jabbed the glowing red tip of the poker into her exposed palm.

The pain was astonishing. A part of her knew she was shrieking and had fallen to her knees on the fine Persian carpet, but the rest of her felt as though she'd been hurled through space and time toward the roaring hearts of a thousand black stars, cosmic furnaces that would consume not just her flesh and bone but her very soul. They would destroy her so completely that no one would remember that she had ever lived. The stars swirled around her, judging her, and she knew they found her lacking. She was too small, unripe, and they cast her back toward Earth. It was the first time and last time she'd ever been glad to be a disappointment in the eyes of the universe.

Tears blurred her vision and through them her father looked strange, distorted. In that instant she was sure that she knelt at the feet of a monstrous stranger who was wearing her father's pallid face as a mask.

"Now, *that* hurts I expect," the stranger observed cheerfully as her flesh sizzled beneath the red iron. "And so I don't expect I shall hear you whining about practice again, will I? Now, stop your little dog howling this instant or I'll burn the other one, too!"

She willed herself to bite back her screams, and he finally let her go just as she passed out from the agony.

When she woke up on the couch, she discovered that her father had fetched some snow from the porch and pressed a grapefruit-sized ball of it into her palm to numb her burn. Icy water dripped down her wrist and soaked her sweater sleeve. The air was filled with the odor of burned meat. Hers. It made her feel even sicker, and for the rest of her life the smell of grilling steaks and chops would make her want to vomit.

Her father gazed down at her, sad and sober.

"I would never hurt you, you understand?" He gently brushed the hair out of her face. "If anyone has hurt you in this world, it was not I."

He bundled her into the back of his Cadillac and took her to see a physician friend of his. Caroline remembered sitting in a chair in the hallway with a handkerchief full of ice in her hand, weeping quietly from the pain while the two men spoke behind a closed door.

"Will her playing be affected?" her father asked.

"Christ, Dunric!" The physician sounded horrified. "Is that your only concern for your own daughter?"

"Of course not!" her father huffed. "Nonetheless, it *is* a concern. So, if you would be so kind as to offer your professional opinion on the matter?"

"She's got a third degree burn; her palm is roasted through like a lamb fillet. I can't see how she could have held on to a live coal so long of her own accord. Are you sure no one else could have been involved? Perhaps a resentful servant?"

"Quite sure," he replied. "My daughter has some...mental peculiarities she regrettably inherited from her mother. You know how unstable sopranos are! Her mother often had a kind of petit mal seizure; I believe some pyromania compelled the girl to take hold of the coal and then a fit prevented her from dropping it as a sensible child would."

"That is unfortunate." The physician sounded unconvinced, and for a brief moment hope swelled in Caroline's heart: perhaps he would challenge her father, investigate further, discover the truth. And then perhaps she'd be sent to live with her mother's people in Boston. She'd only met them once—they were bankers or shoemakers or something else rather dull but they seemed decent enough.

But it was not to be. The physician continued: "Her tendons and ligaments are almost certainly affected. She may need surgery to regain full mobility in her fingers, and I fear that her hand may be permanently drawn due to scarring."

"Well, she only needs to curl it 'round the neck of her instrument, after all."

It took two surgeries to repair the tendons in her hand, and all her father's colleagues marveled at how brave and determined she was in her physical therapy and practice sessions afterward. Her father glowed at the praises they heaped on her, and while he never said as much, something in his smile told her that, should she cease to be so pleasingly dedicated to the musical arts, there were things in his world worse than hot metal.

Caroline traced the lines of her scar with her thumb. The doctor's knife had given it a strange, symbolic look. Some people claimed it resembled a Chinese or Arabic character, although nobody could say which one.

She flexed her hand and shook her head to try to banish the memories. There was no point in dwelling on any of it. Her father was long gone. Five years after he burned her, he'd flown into a rage at a negative review in the newspaper. He drove off in his Alfa Romeo with a bottle of Glenfiddich. Caroline suspected he'd gone to see a ballerina in the next city who enjoyed being tied up and tormented. But he never arrived. He lost control of his car in the foggy hills and his car overturned in a drainage ditch that was hidden from the road. Pinned, he lived for three days while hungry rats gnawed away the exposed flesh of his face, eyes and tongue.

At his funeral, she'd briefly considered quitting music just to spite his memory...but if she refused to be the Maestro's daughter, what was she? She knew nothing of gymnastics or any other sports, nor was she an exceptional student or a skilled painter. Her crabbed hand was nimble on a fingerboard but useful for little else. Worst of all, she knew—since she'd been repeatedly told so—that she was quite plain, good as a violinist but unremarkable as a woman. Her music was the only conceivable reason anyone would welcome her to a wedding. A thousand creditors had picked her father's estate as clean as the rodents had stripped his skull; if she abandoned the violin, what would she have left?

"Caroline, is that you?" Professor Harroe called after she knocked on the door to his office.

"Yes, sir."

"Do come in! I have a bit of a surprise for you today."

She suddenly felt apprehensive, but made herself smile at the professor as she opened the door and took her accustomed seat in the chair in front of his desk, which was stacked high with music theory papers, scores, and books. "What is it?"

He leaned back in his battered wooden swivel chair behind his desk and smiled at her in return. Her anxiety tightened; Harroe had been her music tutor since she was a teenager, and he almost *never* smiled, not at his colleagues' jokes nor at beautiful women nor at lovely music. She searched his face, trying to decipher his expression. He looked practically giddy, she finally decided, and it was a bit unsettling.

"Did you know that your father was working on a series of violin sonatas when he died?"

Her skin itched beneath her sweater. She rubbed at the scar again. "No, I did not."

"He was writing them for you, for when your playing would be mature enough to handle them. He told me he intended them to be a surprise for your 21st birthday. I think he realized his dalliance with drink might lead to disaster—as indeed it sadly did—so he arranged for his lawyer to send me the sonatas along with a formal request that I complete them in secret.

"I regret that I am not half the composer he was, but I am proud to say I have done as he asked. Six months late for your 21st, and for that I apologize, but at last his music is ready for you."

"I...oh my. I really don't know what to say. That was very...kind of you."

"I regret that kindness had nothing to do with it; as a composer I could not pass up the opportunity to co-author a work with the good Maestro. It was an extraordinary challenge, one that I am most pleased I was able to meet. I had to consult with...certain experts to complete the work, and one is here today, ready to listen to you perform the first sonata. If you do well—and I am sure that you will!—I believe that he is prepared to offer you a musical patronage that will ensure that you're taken care of for the rest of your life."

Caroline felt simultaneously numb with surprise and overwhelmed by dread. Was this truly an opportunity to escape her slide into poverty? Few students in her position ever saw salvation arriving before they'd even graduated. She *had* to rise to the occasion. But knowing her father was behind it all made her want nothing more than to go back to her cramped, drafty apartment and hide under the covers.

Her lips moved for a moment before she could get any words out. “That’s amazing, but I couldn’t possibly perform a piece I haven’t even seen—”

“Nonsense!” His tone left her no room for demurral or negotiation. “You are a fine sight-reader, and after all this music is made for you. You’ll be splendid.”

Feeling supremely self-conscious about her dowdy thriftstore clothes and the unfashionable knit cap over her unwashed hair, Caroline took a deep breath, got a better grip on her violin case, lifted her chin, and strode out onto the small, brightly-lit recital stage. Her footsteps echoed hollowly off the curved walls. The theatre was small, just thirty seats, and she could sense rather than clearly see someone sitting in the back row on the left side. Normally having just one listener would bolster her confidence, but today, the emptiness of the room seemed eerie. She bowed crisply toward the dark figure, and then took her seat in a spotlighted wooden folding chair. The music stand held a hand-written musical booklet made from old-fashioned parchment. Her eyes scanned the cover sheet:

Into the Hands of the Living God

An Etude in G Minor for Violin

Composed by Dunric Cage-Satin with Dr. Alexander Harroe

Caroline frowned at the title. Was this some sort of religious music? As far as she knew, her father had been an ardent atheist his entire life. Ah well. There was nothing to do but struggle through as best she could. At worst she’d perform miserably, lose her mysterious patron, and be exactly as penniless as she’d been when she woke up that morning. She opened her violin case, pulled her instrument and bow from the padded blue velvet cutouts, carefully ran her rosin puck across the horsehair, flipped the cover page over to expose the unfamiliar music, and prepared to play.

The notes bore a cold, complex intelligence, and the tonality reminded her a little of Benjamin Britten. But there was something else here, something she’d neither heard nor played before, but nothing bound in stanzas was beyond the capacity of her instrument or her skills. She gave herself over to craft and educated reflex and the stark black notes transubstantiated into soaring music as nerves drove muscle, keratin mastered steel, and reverberation shook maple and spruce.

The stage fell away, and she found herself standing upon a high, barren cliff above a huge lake with driving waves. The air had an unhealthy taint to it, and in the sky there hung a trio of strange, misshapen moons, and opposite the setting twin suns three black stars rose, their bright coronas gleaming through the streaked clouds.

When the dark starlight touched her palm, her scar exploded, a nova made flesh. She fell to her knees on the lichen-covered rocks, unable to even take a breath to scream as the old lines glowed with a transcendent darkness, hot as any stellar cataclysm.

She heard footsteps and the rustling of robes, and through her tears she saw a regal iron boot beneath an ochre hem embroidered with the tiny white bones of birds and mice.

"You'll do," the figure said in a voice that made her want to drive spikes into her own brain. "Yes, you'll do."

She felt the terrible lord touch her head, and it was like being impaled on a sword, and suddenly she was falling—

—Caroline gasped and the bow slipped and screeched across her strings. Blinking in fear and confusion, it took her a half second to realize she was still onstage, still performing...or she had been until her mistake.

"I'm—I'm so, so sorry, I don't know what happened," she stammered, looking to her lone audience member in the back of the theatre. But all the seats were empty.

"It's quite all right." Professor Harroe hurried onstage from the wings, beaming. "You did wonderfully, just wonderfully."

"I...I did?" She blinked at him in disbelief. "But...I messed up, didn't I?"

"Oh, a mere sight-reading error...I'm sure you'll play straight through to the end next time! *And.* Your new benefactor has requested that you perform tomorrow evening at the St. Barnabus Church on 5th Street. 6pm sharp; don't be late!"

"Oh. Yes. Okay." She set her violin down on her lap, and the pain in her hand made her look at her palm. Her scar had split open during the performance, and her sleeve was wet with her own blood.

When Caroline tried to sleep on her narrow bed, she fell almost immediately into a suite of nightmares. She was onstage again, and the notes of her father's sonata turned to tiny hungry spiders that swarmed over her arms and chewed through her eyes and into her brain. Predatory black stars wheeled around her as she tumbled helplessly through airless, frigid outer space. And then she was back in the strange land with the twin suns, but now she was a tiny mouse pinned to a flat rock, and a masked man in yellow robes told her how he would flay her alive and take her spine.

She awoke sweating and weeping at 3am, and in a moment of perfect clarity, she realized that she wanted no part of whatever was happening at St. Barnabus in 15 hours. There was not enough money in the world. She quickly dressed in her secondhand pants and sweater, threw a few belongings into an overnight bag and grabbed her violin case. The Greyhound station was just a mile walk from her apartment building, and there would be a bus going somewhere far away. Maybe she could go to Boston, find her mother's people and learn to make shoes or whatever it was that they did. Shoes were good. People needed shoes.

But when she reached the pitchy street and started striding toward the station, she realized that the city was darker than usual. Tall buildings whose penthouses normally glowed with habitation were entirely black. She scanned the sky: no stars or moon, nothing but a seeming void.

And then, she saw something like a tattered black handkerchief flutter onto a nearby tall streetlamp, blotting it out. She stood very still for a moment, then slowly turned, beholding the uncanny night. Tattered shadows flapped all around. She started running, the violin case banging against her hip. The tatters moved faster, swarming around her on all sides. Soon she was sprinting headlong down the street, across the bridge...

...And realized the other side of the bridge was lost in the ragged blackness. No trace of light; it was as if that part of the world had ceased to exist, had been devoured by one of the stars from her nightmares.

She looked behind her. More utter darkness. The city was blotted out.

"I won't do it," she said, edging toward the bridge railing. She could hear the river rushing below. "I *won't*."

The jagged darkness rapidly ate the bridge, surging toward her, and so she unslung her violin case and hurled her instrument over the edge into the murky water. The darkness came at her even faster, and she crouched down, covering her head with her arms—

—And found herself sitting in a metal folding chair in the nave of a strange church. In her hands was her old violin, the one she'd played as a child. Her father's sonata rested on the music stand before her, the notes black as the predatory stars.

"I won't," she whispered again, but she no longer ruled her own flesh. Her hands lifted her instrument to her shoulder and expertly drew the bow across the strings. The scabbed sign in her palm split open again, ruby blood spilling down her wrist, and she could see the marks starting to shine darkly as they had in the dream. Something planted in her long ago was seeking a way out.

Caroline found her eyes were still under her control, so she looked away from the music, looked out the window, hoping that blinding herself to the notes would stop the performance. But her hands and arms played on, her body swaying to keep time.

And there through the window she saw the glow of buildings on fire, and in the sky she saw a burning version of the symbol in her palm, and the air was rending, space and time separating, and as the firmament tore apart at the seams she could see the twin suns and black stars moving in from the world of her nightmares.

And she wanted to weep, but her body played on.

And the people in the city cried out in fear and madness, and still it played on.

And the winds from Carcosa blew the fires of apocalypse across the land, and still it played on.

The Abomination of Fensmere

On a Saturday exactly one month after her mother died in a car wreck, Penny heard a strange car slow down outside her house and stop. She put down her Nancy Drew novel—*The Moonstone Castle Mystery,* which her mother had bought her only an hour before her death and which Penny kept reading over and over as if somewhere in its pages was the solution to human mortality—and peeked through her second-story bedroom window to see who had arrived.

A gleaming black two-door Oldsmobile F-85 sedan crouched at the curb. Her stepfather took her car shopping the day after the funeral, but she'd refused to take a test ride with him, preferring to sit in a chair at the dealership and read her book. Still, she'd overheard the men's auto talk and knew the model on sight.

A tall balding man in an old-fashioned suit unfolded himself from the driver's seat, pulled an old leather briefcase from the back of the car, and began striding toward the house. He was about her stepfather's age, and had angular features she might have found handsome if it were not for the unsettling intensity of his pale blue eyes and the unpleasant downward cant of his mouth.

He doesn't look like a kind gentleman, she thought.

Penny quietly slipped out of her room and stood just out of sight above the stair landing, listening, watching the dust motes dance in a beam of light from the hallway window. In the distance, her little brother and sisters shrieked and whooped as they played Cowboys and Indians. The doorbell rang.

"Penny, can you get that?" her stepfather called from his first-floor study.

She went perfectly still, not breathing.

"Penny, are you there?"

The stranger rang the bell again, and she heard her stepfather curse under his breath and go to the door.

"Dr. Farrell?" The stranger had a deep voice like a radio announcer.

"Yes?" Her stepfather sounded cautious, tense.

"My name is Ezekias Haughton," he replied smoothly in a peculiar accent. "And I am your stepdaughter Penny's second cousin."

Cousin? Penny wondered. Her mother hadn't ever mentioned any cousins. Or aunts and uncles, for that matter. Until that moment, all the extended family she knew were her stepfather's relatives.

"You have my condolences on your wife Edna's recent tragic death," Haughton continued, "I come here as a representative of her family. I wish to discuss with you certain arrangements for her daughter that will have a salutary impact upon your own finances."

"Salutary...what do you mean?" Her stepfather sounded skeptical. But curious.

"Is the girl here?"

"I think she walked down to the corner store."

"Is there someplace we can chat where we won't be interrupted by your children?" Haughton asked.

"Certainly...come this way to my study."

Penny knew where all the creaky boards in the upstairs hallway floor were. She also knew that if she crouched down in the corner of the upstairs linen closet, she could hear everything anyone so much as whispered inside her stepfather's study. Quickly and quietly, she hurried down the hall and sequestered herself in the sweet spot on the closet floor before the men had settled. She could hear the squeak of her stepfather's office chair and the scrape of the guest chair being pulled out on the other side of his desk.

"I'm sure your wife's death was a dreadful blow to poor Penny," Haughton said, his voice oiled with sympathy.

"It was. It's been a terrible time for all of us." His tone was guarded.

"Girls at her age go through so many difficult changes, even at the best of times. It's hard to be a good father, especially when the girl isn't your own."

"I'm the only father Penny's known, and I've raised her just like my other children," her stepfather replied.

"Please, take no offense, Dr. Farrell! You are an upstanding gentleman and a fine *pater familias*. But, as they say, blood is thicker than water. And adolescent girls are enigmas wrapped in sullen mysteries. No one can argue that."

Penny frowned in the dark, wanting to argue it. While she didn't mind being thought of as mysterious, she disliked it when men lumped girls together as though they were all fish in a can of sardines or cakes on a conveyer belt. Further, she suspected that what Haughton took as girls' mysteries were his own investigative failures.

There was a silence. "Why are you here, Haughton?"

"A girl Penny's age needs a strong maternal presence in her life so that she can grow up to be the fine lady we both know she should be. Her mother's regrettable decision to cut ties with her own parents has meant that Penny has thus far grown up without knowing most of her own kin. I propose that we remedy both problems."

"How?"

"Penny's aunt Morinda wants to have the girl over for a visit at the family home in Fensmere, Mississippi this summer. Say until August."

Her stepfather paused again. "Starting when?"

"I hoped to take the girl back with me today."

"You can't be serious. I'm not handing my daughter over to some stranger who just walked in off the street."

Penny heard the sound of the briefcase's latches popping open. "I have my identification here, and a copy of Morinda's birth certificate, along with your wife's. As you can see, although Morinda is fifteen years your wife's senior, they had the same parents and were born in the same hospital. I know you'll say such documents could be forged, so I have a collection of photographs and newspaper clippings from the town paper that Morinda kept. Look there; your wife was an accomplished pianist in her youth. She and Morinda even played a concert together at the governor's mansion; there's a picture here."

For several minutes, Penny heard nothing but the distant shuffling of paper and photos. She drifted into daydreams as she imagined a younger version of her mother playing to an adoring audience on *American Bandstand.*

"All right," her stepfather finally said. "I believe you are who you claim to be. But it's ridiculous to think that Penny could leave for such a long stay on such short notice!"

"I do realize it's sudden, and an inconvenience, but Morinda wishes to compensate you for your trouble."

There came the sound of a weighty packet dropping on the desk.

"What's this?" her stepfather asked.

"It's enough to cover the debt you owe to...certain parties in New Jersey."

Her stepfather inhaled in surprise. "How do you know about that?"

"Oh, dear Doctor, please don't look so alarmed. Every man has his vice, and many gentlemen gamble. You simply had a run of poor luck. Family of Penny's is family of ours, and family secrets are safe with us. Your patients and neighbors will never have to know of this unfortunate footnote in your life, nor about your somewhat *unsavory* dalliances with the carnival boys...provided my dear young cousin can leave with me late this afternoon."

Penny shivered at the threats swimming like hungry sea monsters beneath the surface of Haughton's voice. She couldn't sort out what Haughton meant by "unsavory dalliances," but she was not in the least shocked to find out that her stepfather had not been spending all his time at his downtown office as he'd claimed. Her mother's tone and manner were strained on the evenings he was late, and when he got home he was just too nice to everyone. She'd known all along something was afoot.

"What...what do I tell her? How do you expect me to explain this?" Her stepfather's voice was tight as a violin string.

"Her fourteenth birthday is next week, is it not? Tell her that summer vacation at her long-lost aunt's house is a surprise present. Tell her she will be greeted there with cakes and the freshest peach ice cream. Girls love peaches."

Penny almost vowed to hate peaches from that moment forward on general principle. But then she remembered how much she liked Peach Melba and abandoned the idea.

There was another long pause.

"All right."

"Excellent. There are a few papers I need you to sign to ensure that Morinda can act *in loco parentis....*"

Penny's heart beat loud in her ears, drowning out Haughton's voice. Part of her told her to grab a few books and clothes, duck out the window, climb down the tree and run away. But where would she go? Her only good friend at school,

Susan, was already off at summer camp. Any of her stepfather's relatives would surely just hand her back to him, as would the neighbors.

Another, louder voice in her mind reminded her that staying at home promised a long, tedious summer of nothing much to do but babysit her little half-siblings while Dr. Farrell worked or indulged himself. And besides, there were enticing mysteries afoot. What was her Aunt Morinda like? Was she anything like Penny's mother? Did she have a nice house? If she was paying her stepfather a lot of money, it *must* be a nice house. Penny briefly imagined herself sliding down the banister in some grand old manor and wandering in a rose garden, searching for clues to some family mystery.

What would Nancy Drew do? Clearly, the girl detective wouldn't flinch from adventure. Penny slipped out of the closet to start packing for the journey.

Once he'd loaded Penny and her luggage into his Oldsmobile, Haughton was even less cheerful than he'd seemed at a distance, and he'd apparently exhausted his supply of conversation with her stepfather. Worse, he smelled of mothballs and cellar must. But Penny was content to curl up in the back seat with her book. After just an hour, the hum of the tires on the highway lulled her to sleep.

When she awoke in the heat of the morning sun, she discovered that he had driven straight through the night. She sat up, rubbed her eyes, and gazed out the windows, wondering how she'd managed to snooze through Haughton's fuel stops. They passed neat rows of downtown stores: a Woolworth's, a soda shop, a hairdresser's, a diner.

Her stomach rumbled when she saw a man step out of the diner with a half-eaten turnover pastry. He shoved the remaining piece into his mouth and chewed it mechanically, expressionless, his eyes staring out at something so far away that Penny had no chance of spying it.

"I'm hungry; may we stop for breakfast?" she asked.

"Your aunt will have a fine meal waiting for you at her house." His tone made it clear there was no room for negotiation.

She was suddenly aware of an intense pressure in her bladder. "Please, I need a restroom."

"Of course." He pulled off at a nearby filling station and hovered near the door while she used the cramped women's facilities.

Afterward, they drove on in silence. Penny watched the townspeople in their Sunday best walking along the concrete promenade. Something about their countenances unsettled her. It wasn't that they all looked unnaturally pale in a place where the sun beat down so ruthlessly, nor was it that they all seemed to have the same dust-colored hair that fringed Haughton's balding pate, his same sharp features. It was the expressions on their faces that sent a chill into her marrow: every person she saw, even the few children, looked so grim that she imagined none of them had experienced a single bit of joy in their entire lives.

"What do the people do here?" she asked.

"Many are farmers or mill hands. Others are craftsmen, shopkeepers. The same as anyplace else."

"No, I mean...what do they do for fun?" The moment she spoke, she realized that this was not a favored word in her cousin's vocabulary.

"Our town is devout and we don't have time for juvenile nonsense," he replied. "But many folks enjoy our church dances. Those are...*fun*, I think."

"What about concerts?" she asked, once again imagining her mother playing piano on TV.

"Oh, we haven't had concerts here in over a decade. Not since your—not since the theatre burned down."

At least there's dancing, she thought, feeling suffocated in the over-warm car. Not that it would do her much good; she'd never learned any good steps, and the school dances she'd attended had been boring exercises in watching the popular boys and girls show off for each other. She wished she'd thought to bring her record player and her albums; a whole summer without a single Beach Boys song seemed grim indeed! But, she reflected, her aunt certainly had a radio, and there was always television.

Haughton drove through the rest of the town and down a long road lined with tall pines. He turned off onto a long driveway paved in blacktop that opened onto a roundabout in front of what Penny could only think of as a genuine mansion. The three-story house had to be at least three times the size of her parents' ranch house, and the front bore double porches supported by thick, whitewashed columns. In the middle of the roundabout grew a large magnolia with pink, fleshy blossoms that attracted a profusion of bees and flies.

"Here we are," said Haughton. "A servant will be along to get your things."

Penny expected someone like a British butler to emerge from the massive brass-fitted front doors, but instead, a slim teenaged girl with black braids and caramel-colored skin slipped outside and padded toward the car. She wore a simple sleeveless daisy print shift, and her left wrist and forearm were in a plaster cast.

"Oh," Penny said, staring at the girl's injured arm as Haughton unlocked the trunk. "It's okay; I can get my own bags."

"She'll do her job if she wants to be paid." Haughton scowled down at the girl.

"Yessir!" Not meeting his gaze, the girl slung the medium-sized bag across her body, tucked the smallest under her injured arm, and hauled out the big suitcase with her right.

"I'll take you to your room, Miss Penny." Her back, legs, and shoulders straining with obvious effort, the girl stumbled toward the door. Feeling awkward and mortified, Penny trailed behind, following the girl into the house. The girl led her past a huge staircase with a banister too ornately carved to slide upon, through a hallway and into a large, high-ceilinged bedroom dominated by a massive four-posted mahogany bed. The walls were painted an icy white, and the two narrow windows wore heavy maroon drapes half-closed to block out the morning sun.

Sweating in the cool air, the girl carefully set the luggage down on the floor. "Your bathroom's through there, Miss Penny." She inclined her head toward a small door that Penny had taken to be a closet.

"Are you okay?" Penny asked when the girl doubled over, leaning onto her knees.

"I'm fine, Miss Penny." The girl straightened up, smiling although she was obviously still in pain.

"It's just Penny. You really don't have to call me 'Miss.'" She'd thought it would be fancy to have a servant call her "Miss," but now that it was happening, it just felt uncomfortable, like trying to wear a formal dress tailored for some other girl.

"Miz Rinda wouldn't like it if I didn't address you proper."

"What's your name?"

"Bessie. Bessie Turner."

Penny brightened. Bess Marvin was one of Nancy Drew's best friends; perhaps this was a sign? "It's good to meet you, Bessie!"

The girl eyed her, still smiling dutifully. "Uh…good to meet you too, Miss Penny."

"So, how did you hurt your arm?"

Bessie's smile faded. "I said something I shouldn't have, and Miz Rinda didn't like it."

"...what?" Penny goggled at her in shock.

A sudden realization sparked in the girl's eyes, and she smiled and shook her head as if she'd made a joke. "Oh, pay me no mind! Ain't nothing! My mama's setting the table right now, and Miz Rinda says she wanted me to make sure you join her for breakfast. I put some fresh towels out for you in the bathroom if you want to wash up. Please pull the cord by the door if you need anything; it'll ring a bell downstairs and I'll come up right quick." The words spilled out of her, panic clear in her tone if not on her face. "I need to go help Mama with breakfast. Bye now!"

The girl curtsied awkwardly and ran from the room.

Penny blinked after her. The room was suddenly oppressively quiet.

Face and arms washed and changed into a fresh cotton dress, Penny went downstairs and found the dining room. It held a dark wood table big enough to hold a dozen people, but the only person who was seated there was a thin, elderly woman with a regal bearing who—after the girl's eye was able to move past her wild mane of white hair and her sagging, spotted skin—Penny realized bore a striking resemblance to her dead mother.

Even the dead part, she thought to herself. *Though surely she was quite lovely when she was young.*

And then, a more alarming thought: *Will I look like* that *when I'm old?*

"Ah, child, you've come down to join us." The grand old lady speared her silver-topped cane on the floor and pushed herself to her feet. She stood an imposing head taller than Penny. "Come give your Auntie Rinda a kiss hello!"

Stomach tightening, Penny made herself smile, stepped forward, stood on tiptoes, and planted a light kiss on her aunt's powdered cheek. Like Haughton, the old lady smelled of mothballs and mold, although her lavender perfume nearly overwhelmed the odor.

"Ah, my child." Morinda held Penny at arms' length. "You look so much like your dear mother. You have the stars in your eyes, just like her! But, alas, you're short like your father."

It was hard to keep herself from frowning; nobody had called Penny short before, and she didn't care for it. And Morinda had pronounced "father" in the same tone as most people said "maggot" or "rat."

Bessie and an older, chubby woman with skin the color of molasses—she had to be the girl's mother—were bustling back and forth bringing dishes from the kitchen. It took Penny a moment to notice that the woman had a black eye. She was wondering where Bessie's mother had gotten her bruise when she realized that there was a third place setting on the table.

"Is Mr. Haughton joining us?" she asked.

"Well, bless your heart!" Morinda released her and sat back down in her chair. "No, Ezekias is attending to church business today. We always leave a place at the table for my brother, the Reverend; he's long been afflicted with a sleeping sickness he caught on an expedition in Arabia, but we hope that the warmer weather will help his blood along and he'll join us one of these days soon."

"An expedition?" Penny asked, still standing.

Bessie hurried around the table and pulled Penny's chair out; feeling uncomfortable again, she sat and the servant girl pushed her close to the table.

"Yes; Eleazar is an expert in certain mysteries, and they needed him to identify relics in a ruined city amongst the dunes. The journey was a spiritual revelation to him, but sadly took a toll on his health. His rooms are on the third floor; it's important to preserve his rest, so nobody is allowed up there unless I can supervise them myself. We have strict rules here at Haughton Manor to prevent noise that might disturb him. No horseplay, no raised voices, no hammering or sawing near the house, no music."

"What about television?"

Morinda looked aghast. "My word! We would *never* allow an idiot box in this house!"

Stunned, Penny stared down at her plate as Bessie opened a biscuit upon it and ladled gravy across the halves. No *Lassie*? No Walt Disney? No *Bonanza*? No Alfred Hitchcock? No *Man from U.N.C.L.E*? How would she survive the summer in such isolation?

"I trust you'll enjoy your breakfast, dear," her aunt said, oblivious to Penny's dismay. "Georgia cooks it *exactly* according to Haughton family recipes. Don't you, Georgia?"

"Yes'm, I do," the woman replied, her voice cautious rather than proud.

Penny's mother's biscuits were light and flaky; these were thick and dense. The gravy was heavy, and even warm it had an unpleasant gelatinous feel in her mouth and left a strange, bitter aftertaste. She dutifully ate what was on her plate.

"Have some cantaloupe, dear; it's fresh from the garden! And try the peaches!"

The cantaloupe, which was more beige than orange, had grainy texture and was cloyingly sweet. The peaches looked ripe enough, but they were sour, and the cream had the same bitterness as the gravy. Even a spoonful of sugar didn't help.

After breakfast, a man with a black physician's bag arrived at the house; he bore a striking resemblance to Mr. Haughton. After a hushed exchange in the foyer, Morinda took him upstairs, presumably to examine the Reverend.

Penny went into the kitchen, where Bessie was drying dishes with a white rag and her mother was putting pots and pans away in the cupboards.

"Did you need something, child?" Georgia asked. Sweat was beaded on her brow.

"I was wondering if Bessie could play cards with me. Later, I mean, when she isn't busy. You could play, too, if you wanted?"

"Oh, bless your heart!" Georgia said. "We'll be busy here right up until we need to walk into town to catch the last bus back to Bucktown."

"Walk?" Penny asked. It had to be at least three miles back to town! "It's so hot out there; can't Mr. Haughton give you a ride?"

Bessie gave a bitter laugh, and her mother shot her a look.

"Child, don't you say a word; you want a cast on the other one, too?"

"No'm." Bessie went back to her drying.

"I think if you stayed, and if I asked nicely, Mr. Haughton would give you a ride?"

"Bless your heart." Georgia shook her head and gave Penny an appraising look. "I reckon you really ain't from around here, are you? You ever met a Negro before?"

Penny thought hard, realized the brief interactions she'd had with porters and hotel maids didn't really count, and shook her head. "No, ma'am."

"How you reckon my folk live 'round here?"

"Like...folks?" she replied.

At their expressions of disbelief, she added: "Am I...missing something?" She felt as though she'd walked into a terrible, incomprehensible situation.

"Miss Penny." Georgia inhaled through her nose, clearly trying to figure out how to phrase some harsh truth. "Our folks ain't welcome in Fensmere 'cept as help, and *only* as help. Back when the slaves got freed, the town fathers declared that no Negroes could be about after dark. If we're inside the town limits come sundown, we're likely to be hanging by our necks from a roadside tree come sunup."

Penny stared at her in open-mouthed horror.

"Miz Rinda says help from the two of us is worth five round dollars a day," said Bessie, "And even that's a cruel robbery of her family fortune. Getting ourselfs home is none of her concern."

Penny remembered the prices at the Oldsmobile dealership and realized that Bessie and her mother could probably *never* afford their own car. They'd have to walk forever. She felt sick at the injustice of it. "I'm sorry."

"Don't worry yourself about it, child," said Georgia. "We're grateful for the work; we ain't starvin', and we ain't in a field all day. And besides, even if we *were* welcome, I can't imagine the money that would make me want to spend a night in Fensmere."

Bereft of television, records and card partners, Penny spent time unpacking and exploring her room. The room was large and well appointed, but dull. No books or old clothes to play dress-up in. The only oddity she discovered was a small, hinged hatch set into the bottom of the sturdy bedroom door, like a door for a cat, but it was wider and only half the height of the pet exits she'd seen.

She couldn't imagine Morinda would allow a small yappy dog, but maybe there was a cat in the house? She loved petting the neighbors' kitties. So, as was her habit at home, she started quietly making her way downstairs, testing for squeaky boards as she stepped, when she overheard the physician and her aunt talking in the foyer. Penny froze at the sound of their voices, listening with sharpened ears.

"So you think he'll be awake by the new moon?" her aunt asked, her voice barely above a whisper.

"Well before then, I'd say. He should be in fine fettle for church."

"Oh, thank the Great One."

"How is the girl?" the physician asked.

"Far less fiery and strong-willed than her mother, to my eye. Ezekias says she went with him without complaint. Polite and compliant the whole trip down. A perfect little lady."

"Good, good."

Morinda sighed. "I don't understand where we went wrong with Edna. Her blood was as pure as we could make it, and yet she resisted us at every turn. And she went and bred with a *Jew*, of all things, after all we taught her! I reckoned Penny would be an utter waste, and yet she seems perfect."

"There are some who extol the benefits of hybrid vigor," the physician replied. "Perhaps the Haughton genes were most able to come to the fore when they had lesser genes to work against?"

Lesser genes? Penny frowned. She couldn't remember her biological father, but her mother told her stories and showed her photos. He'd been handsome, the captain of his college basketball team despite his stature—he enjoyed a challenge, apparently—and later a rising nuclear physicist who died from accidental radiation exposure. She'd seen a letter from the President himself declaring her father's research to be that of a genius. What greater genes did these Haughtons have? She doubted any of them could shoot a single hoop or walk three miles to the bus stop in the summer heat, much less solve a complex equation.

The doctor departed. Calling for Georgia, Morinda swept towards the kitchen. Penny let out her breath and continued down the stairs. A turn of the corner took her to a huge library with floor-to-ceiling shelves and a pair of red wing-backed chairs separated by a reading table.

A large, old, leather-bound book covered with odd symbols lay upon the table. Curious, Penny opened it, and began to read.

An Arab storyteller wrote it, and at first she thought it was some variant of *One Thousand and One Nights.* But in its convoluted prose, she found not tales of princes and thieves but a purported history of strange, unfathomably powerful beings beyond the stars. The narrative drew her in, and she felt the hairs on her arms rise and her heart begin to pound as words describing cosmic grotesqueries few humans could ever come to grips with burned their way through her retina into her brain.

Penny's young mind floundered, drowning in the dark sea of this horrible ancient knowledge. She stumbled back from the book, her chest constricted, and fainted dead away upon the Oriental carpet.

She awoke later in the guest bed. The physician and her aunt loomed over her.

"Ah, she's awake!" he declared. "No worse for wear, eh child?"

"What...what happened?" she sat up, feeling sick and dizzy. She wondered how she had gotten into her nightgown.

"Your blood is thick from living up north and your system isn't accustomed to the heat and humidity," the physician replied smoothly. "You just need to take it easy and not exert yourself."

Bessie came into the room with a bamboo bed tray. Her face was a neutral mask, and she seemed to avoid making eye contact with anyone in the room.

"Drink some tea and eat some pudding," the physician said as Bessie set the tray across her lap.

She ate a few spoonfuls of the overly sweet rice pudding from a glass custard bowl and drank the tepid, bitterly herbal tea from its dainty bone china cup. Soon, her head began to swim, and no matter how hard she tried, her eyelids wouldn't stay open.

"There, that's it, a young girl needs her rest," Penny heard Morinda say just before she passed out.

Penny's dreams took her through the gallery of monstrosities she'd read about in the Arab's book. She tumbled through the cold void of outer space as huge malign creatures lurking in the shadows twixt the burning stars eyed her as a scientist might gaze upon the tiniest itching mite. One brushed her with an enormous icy pseudopod and suddenly she was plummeting down, down through time and space, striking cold misted water and plunging to a crushing depth where she lay trapped in sucking mud, thinking she would drown there alone when the enormous clammy bulk of *something* dragged itself from a chasm nearby and reached out toward her with slimy suckered tentacles—

—she jerked awake in her bed, her nightgown sodden with sweat, heart thudding in her chest, her throat aching as though she had been screaming. She was alone, the room silent, and in that moment she wished she were back home where her mother would always hold her and rock her back to sleep after a nightmare.

And then she remembered her mother was gone, nothing left of her but an urn of ashes buried out in Greenlawn Cemetery, and Penny's heart broke for the hundredth time that month. Why would the universe let someone so beautiful and kind as her mother die so senselessly? The girl wept into her pillow for what felt like an eternity, and still no one came to comfort her.

Finally, she wiped her tears from her eyes, and stumbled into the bathroom to wash her face and brush the sour fuzz from her teeth. She dried herself and stared at her red-eyed reflection. Babies lay in bed and cried, and she wasn't a baby, was she? Sherlock Holmes never cried. Her mother was gone, burned to almost nothing, and what now? What would Nancy Drew do? Why, she'd pick herself up and get on with solving the mystery, wouldn't she?

She inhaled, trying to clear her foggy head, trying to push away the horrible images from her dreams, trying to stop remembering the smell of the funeral home. The Haughtons were not the kind of people who did something out of the goodness of their hearts. They'd brought Penny to their house for a reason. Why? And what was *really* going on in the third floor? Was the Reverend really a sleep-sickened invalid, or were the physician and Morinda keeping him there against his will?

Suddenly Penny felt completely awake, her heart beating quickly again. Her whole body shivered with dread and the desire to go upstairs and see for herself. She put on her robe and slippers, and quietly slipped from her room.

Penny pressed her eye to the bedroom's keyhole. There was an unmoving lump in the bed, barely visible in the moonlight coming through the window. A sleeping man, or just mounded bedclothes? The itch to know was unbearable.

She turned the knob, expecting it to be locked, but the mechanism clicked open and the door swung inward, silent on oiled hinges. She took a cautious step forward into the room, dreading a squeaky floorboard, and then another.

"Child...." the voice was deep and oratorical.

She froze like a deer and turned her head. A gaunt figure sat in the shadowed chair in the corner of the room. It stood and came forward, entering the moonlight, and what she beheld would be burned into her memory forever.

The Reverend was tall and so thin she could see the lumps in his sternum beneath his taut skin. Her eye traveled down his naked torso to his belly, where...

her mind reeled at what she saw. The skin of his abdomen had eroded away, and instead of intestines and other vitals, a vile, crab-armed creature crouched in the basket of his hipbones. A gleaming black head on a long, snaky neck pushed past the tattered curtain of skin and craned toward her. Five eyes faceted like a fly's beheld her with cold curiosity. It chittered at her, a weird cricket chirp that felt like cold fingers scratching up her spine.

"Has your mind been opened to the stars, child?" The Revered intoned, and she realized the vile thing in his belly was controlling him as though he were some Mechanical Turk. "Do you bleed?"

Penny had seen more than enough. She bolted from the room, raced back down the hall and half ran, half tumbled down the stairs. The huge front doors were locked, and she became so focused on undoing the bolts and latches that she did not realize that someone had come up behind her until the ether-soaked rag was pressed tight to her face.

"Now, child," Morinda admonished as Penny tried to fight free. "Be a good girl and this will all be over soon...."

Penny awoke some time later; her head pounded and she felt sicker than when she'd caught stomach flu. She staggered from the bed into the bathroom and dry-heaved into the toilet. The daylight streaming through the window made her eyes ache. She drank water from the tap, washed her face, and tottered back into the bedroom. At least someone had thought to pull all the drapes closed, so the room was comfortably dim. She tried the bedroom door; it was locked from the outside.

A sudden squeak and beam of light at her feet made her look down. Someone had pulled open the little hatch in the bottom of the door.

"Miss Penny, are you awake?" asked Bessie. "I brought you some food."

Penny dropped to her knees, trying to peer out the hatch. All she could see was a tray bearing a teacup and a bowl of porridge and, beyond it, Bessie's scuffed brown Mary Janes.

"Please help me," Penny whispered. "I need to get out of here."

"I...I can't."

"Please! Please, just...call my stepfather and let him know what happened? I can give you the number."

"There ain't no phones here. And if someone was to come looking for you or if you was to go missing, they'd know I had a hand in it. And then it'd be more than a broken arm for me and Mama, you understand? They might burn Bucktown."

Penny was silent. She wanted to weep, but her eyes felt dry as sand.

"I wish I could help you, I really do," Bessie continued. "You seem like a real nice girl. I wish we could have played cards sometime. I'm sorry this is happenin', I really am. But I caint stop it."

"What can I do?"

"Drink the tea. It'll help you sleep. Mama made it real strong."

"Will I die?" Penny whispered.

"We all gonna die. Just a matter of when."

As Bessie promised, the tea was strong, and quickly took Penny back into her cosmic nightmares. They were so compelling and so vivid that, when Penny awoke to find that she had been bound to a wooden cross and men in white robes with pointed white hoods were carrying her amid torchlight toward an old stone church, she at first thought she was surely still dreaming.

But the smoke from the torches made her eyes water, and the leather manacles and straps bit into her wrists, armpits, and ankles; she realized she never felt that sort of mundane physical discomfort in her phantasms. The Klansmen's procession solemnly bore her up the front steps and into the church, which was full of more white-hooded figures standing on bleachers from the floor to rafters along the walls. Flickering torches and wrought iron candelabras cast strange shadows throughout the whole room. The Reverend Haughton stood beside a stone altar in front of a large, round stained glass window depicting the same weird symbols she'd seen on the Arab's book, which lay upon the altar in front of him. He wore deep-purple satin robes with a dragon embroidered on the chest. The legs of his operator moved beneath the fabric at his belly.

"Brothers, place her beneath the stars!" the Reverend ordered.

They tilted the cross and slid the post into a slanted hole in the stone floor. She found herself staring up through an open skylight into the cloudless night, the stars a profusion of cold sparks. One of the masked men pulled out another strap and secured her head to the cross so that she could look nowhere else.

"Brothers and sisters of the Invisible Empire!" The Reverend's voice was like that of a god. "We gather here tonight to witness a new chapter for our world. Tonight ends this age of debasement and decadence, this age in which we have seen the sickly fruits of miscegenation and a society threatened by the mud peoples. Communist Orientals, cunning Jews, savage Redskins and brutish Negroes—after tonight, the world will be purified, purged of their stink and disease!"

The crowd of Klansmen and women roared their approval.

"I offer my own dearest flesh and blood, my own granddaughter, as an offering to the Great One. If she is deemed to be the example of exemplary young womanhood we know she is, she shall be the instrument of our salvation from a world of depravity!"

"Halleluja!" she heard Morinda shout from a nearby row.

Granddaughter? Penny wondered. The relationship calculation was simple enough, but it made her feel ill just the same.

She didn't have long to dwell on it, for she heard the ancient book creak open, and the Reverend began to read aloud some abominable incantation that was never meant for human ears. Her mind reeled in terror, and the merciless stars bored down into her eyes.

Penny felt her consciousness travel up, up into darkness as it did in her nightmares, only it was all real now, and she felt the vast consciousness of the eternal entity known to humans as Yog-Sothoth turn to notice her.

How many miserable souls live upon your petty world? Its voice was a blowtorch upon the wax of her sanity, but the hardened bits of her mind summoned up the figure from her nearly-forgotten geography class.

"Three billion, two hundred sixty-three million," she whispered.

A pittance. Not worth leaving my lair. Yog-Sothoth turned away from her and went back to observing the collapse of a nearby nebula.

Behind the ancient Old One, Penny sensed a throng of its dark minions clamoring to taste what their master scorned as unripe fruit. She turned and beheld her own planet as they did: an insignificant backwater world populated by craven, base gangs of over-proud apes...and none, perhaps, quite so abominable as the hooded figures who surrounded her body in the church.

In the back of her mind, she could hear the Reverend's incantation intensify, and she felt the power of the stars themselves flood into her soul, her mind. Penny realized that she was the goddess of all who existed or who would ever exist on planet Earth, the ultimate Angel of Death for a species that seemed as eternally doomed and insignificant as a nest of ants in some forgotten desert. She could end all the pointless struggle and war and striving with a single thought, and the human race would become fuel for the beings who were by far their cosmic superiors.

The cosmic energy flowing into her was enough to open a portal in the stained glass window and allow the hungry minions to swarm across the countryside, first toward Bucktown, and then the rest of the world.

Dost thou wish it? Asked the minions.

The human animal in her—the part of her that wanted to jump when she found herself at great heights, the part that delighted when misfortune befell the bullies at her school—that part wanted to tell them "yes" and open the portal.

Why should they survive when Mother is dust? it asked her.

But another part, the part that was capable of performing demanding music and the coldest of equations, the part that would not gibber in terror no matter what horrors the old gods showed her, had a better idea.

"I do not wish it."

The minions turned away, indifferent, Penny instantly forgotten.

Penny closed her eyes against the stars and let the power of the Reverend's spell explode out of her every pore. Her body became a temporary sun. She heard the Reverend's keeper shriek a moment before it was incinerated along with its puppet. The Klan members had no time to scream before they burst into ash along with the wood and rock of the church.

When Penny opened her eyes, she found herself lying on her back at the bottom of a blasted, scorched crater, her cosmic energies spent. Nothing but she had survived.

The Girl With the Star-Stained Soul

Dazed, Penny stumbled through the gray ash and blasted debris. Charred human fat stained the fractured rocks of the old stone church. Blackened bones jumbled with the splintered charcoal of the pine roof beams. Most all the men of Fensmere, Mississippi lay dead around her, and many of its womenfolk, too. She spied a bit of wrought iron candelabra here, a burned scrap of a Klansman's hood there.

She looked up at the broken wall where the skylight had been, and the Reverend Haughton's order reverberated in her mind: *"Brothers, place her beneath the stars!"*

The girl shuddered and hugged herself as she remembered the cold touch of the old gods probing her mind, examining the Earth through her memory and dismissing her world as unripe fruit. But their thronging dark minions had clamored to devour the planet, and Penny had seen through the old gods' eyes what terrible, craven, worthless creatures humankind was, and the darkest power of the cosmos had flowed into her, and she could have opened the doorway to let the minions in to end it all.

And for a moment, she'd considered it. It's what the Reverend—her own grandfather—had brought her here to do. Exactly a month after Penny's mother's death, the Reverend's sister brought her to the family mansion for the summer under the guise of a family reunion. Instead, the Haughtons wrenched her mind open with the mad Arab's book, drugged her and kept her penned like a sacrificial calf until the night that the stars were right.

And she'd almost done it. She'd almost opened the door and let in creatures that would almost certainly end humanity. In those moments, she'd been the most powerful person on the planet, a living goddess, and yet still nothing more than a child trying to decide whether to open the latch for the stranger on her parents' porch.

Instead, she'd chosen to use the cosmic power surging through her to turn her body into a momentary sun. And with the coldest blood, she blasted the Invisible Empire cultists gathered around her to ashes.

Penny couldn't stop shivering. Her own mind had been overlaid with a new dark consciousness, a terrible inhuman logic. Was she a puppet now? A servant of one of the old gods that had briefly gazed upon her as a man might gaze upon a mote of dust? No, she finally decided. Her mind had been left to its own devices. But the cosmic fires had forged her soul into something new, and she was a stranger to herself.

And in that moment of realization, two things occurred to her simultaneously.

The first was that the Haughtons had almost certainly engineered her mother's fatal automobile crash. It could be no accident that the one adult in her life who'd kept her safe had been removed right when Penny was old enough for the ritual. They had the money and resources to make it happen, and it had been done. Her cold new overmind shone a light on her past, and Penny realized they'd probably arranged to have her father murdered, too.

The second thing Penny realized was that, had her nuclear physicist father lived, and had her mother not remarried a Christian man when Penny was just a toddler, she might be having her bat mitzvah this summer instead. Her parents would have thrown her a big party with cake and Peach Melba and all the friends Penny didn't have in her current life would have come to celebrate her becoming a daughter of the commandment under Jewish tradition. And her father would have given thanks that he could no longer be punished for her sins.

"I'm responsible now," she said to the dead who lay scattered around her, and she threw back her head and laughed, spinning in circles with her arms outstretched in the cold moonlight. "I'm responsible for everything!"

She spun and laughed and laughed and spun amongst the dust and bones and soon she was wailing, weeping to the stars that hung deaf and mute and harsh.

"Miss Penny!" a woman exclaimed.

The girl stopped spinning, blinking in bright headlights, and wiped at the muddy tracks her tears had made in the ashes on her cheeks.

"Who's there?" she called back.

Three figures stepped out of an old Hudson sedan, and when they came into the light she recognized Georgia and her daughter Bessie, both servants at the Haughton's mansion. The third was a strong-looking man a few years younger than Georgia, and they looked enough alike in face and build that Penny guessed they were kin. Penny knew Georgia and Bessie couldn't afford a car, so she guessed the truck belonged to him.

"Who are you?" she asked him.

"Name's Jay. I'm—I'm Georgia's brother." He was staring at his battered work boot, clearly averting his gaze. It was only then that Penny realized that her dress had been burned off in the blast.

The Klan would lynch any Negroes found in Fensmere after dark, so Georgia and her family had taken a terrible risk coming to the old stone church...unless they'd been pretty sure the Klansmen were all dead. Penny guessed that blowing up the church made a bit of noise.

"Miss Penny, oh my goodness, where are your clothes?" Georgia fussed. "Bessie, go get the blanket!"

"Yes'm."

"But naked's better than dead, isn't that right?" Penny asked, fixing Georgia in a pointed stare, remembering the cups of drugged tea that Bessie had slipped through the food slot during her imprisonment in the mansion. "You knew damned well they meant for me to die here. And you didn't do anything to stop them."

"Miss Penny, I know you're angry." Georgia's voice shook. "But understand, we did as much as we could. Morinda can't be bothered to do nothin' on her own—she had me brew up the tea and I changed the recipe so your mind would be able to stand everything they put you through. I know we still put you in harm's way...but if we'd done more they'd have found out and lynched me and Bessie and probably burned a few houses in Bucktown as a warning."

"Changed it?" Penny replied, remembering the medicinal bitterness of the tea.

Bessie padded up with an old cotton blanket. Penny took it and wrapped it around herself.

"How did you know to change it?" Penny asked.

"This ain't the first time the Haughtons did this. They tried it with your momma back when she was just a few years older than you. A hoodoo woman from New Orleans come up to warn us what they planned to do, and she showed me what herbs to switch in and out. Your momma was able to hold off the star-devils when they put her on the cross, and we reckoned that if we made the tea right and said our prayers, you'd do the same."

The old theatre downtown, Penny thought. *So* that's *how it burned down.*

"Is the Reverend dead?" Georgia asked, looking anxious. "We need to know. If that evil old buzzard survived—"

"My grandfather is dead. Aunt Morinda, too," Penny replied. "Come see."

She led them over to a blasted corpse that still wore purple silk tatters of a Grand Dragon's robes. The fractured remains of a black, crablike creature still nested in his hipbones. Just as dead as the Reverend.

"Oh Jesus, what's that?" Bessie breathed, and her uncle muttered a prayer under his breath.

Georgia inhaled sharply but didn't react in terror like the other two; Penny figured that the older woman had either seen the abomination, or had guessed that it existed.

"It controlled him like a puppeteer," Penny said. "But I think he was perfectly willing to be used by it."

She turned to Georgia. "You said my mother wouldn't open a portal to the stars?"

Georgia shook her head. "She shut 'em down like you did. Only she just set a fire, and most everyone escaped."

"Then where did this thing come from?" Penny asked.

"I reckon he didn't have it before he went on that expedition in Arabia and came back with all those relics, like that evil book they left for you to find," Georgia replied.

"We better check the house," Penny replied, staring down at the broken black shell and curled arachnoid legs. "The thing about spiders and cockroaches is that if you see one, there's almost always another one somewhere."

Georgia nodded. "I recollect the movers brought in a lot of big crates, and they took them down to the basement. Morinda forbade me from going down there. I didn't want a caning so I never disobeyed her, but I know where she hides the key."

*

Early the next morning, Georgia let the four of them into the musty old mansion. Penny wore a clean shift and pair of Mary Janes she'd borrowed from Bessie. Jay carried a burlap sack laden with pry bars, rope, matches, candles, and a couple of flashlights.

"The Sherriff and his deputies were all Klan," she said as she shut the heavy oak doors behind them. "So I reckon they died at the church along with everything else. Everybody in Bucktown knows to sit tight. But some of the Fensmere womenfolk got left at home with their kids; sooner or later the state police will come 'round here asking questions. So we best find what we gonna find before then."

Nobody, it seemed, wanted to go to the cellar right away. So they went up to the Reverend's rooms on the third floor and searched every closet, drawer, and wardrobe. They found nothing out of the ordinary but some strange and oddly cold figurines carved from black stone. Every time Penny touched one, her mind flashed back on some horror she'd glimpsed among the stars.

"I think we have to go to the basement," Penny said, trying to work the feeling back into her numbed fingers.

Once they descended the long, curving staircase, they found themselves in a hidden warehouse beneath the mansion. Old-fashioned gaslights guttered in sconces on the walls. Penny surveyed the boxes and old furniture with dismay; almost any number of creatures could be hiding down here.

But she realized that the hairs were standing up on the backs of her arms, and she could feel a low humming vibration from somewhere further into the basement. Penny led the others toward the faint sound, and they found an ancient Middle Eastern temple built from blocks and columns of black basalt crouched on the concrete floor. It was maybe fifteen feet tall, the peak of the terraced roof nearly flush with the basement ceiling, and probably twenty feet wide along each side.

The only thing upon it that was not a flat, oppressive black was a single bronze door at the top of a short flight of steps. Upon the gleaming metal was some strange symbol wrought from shining gold. When she gazed upon it, Penny shivered as she had amongst the dead cultists at the old stone church, and she guessed that whatever language it was written in was not one humans could comprehend.

"This thing gives me the heebie-jeebies," Jay said as they carefully circled the temple.

"They must have brought it in pieces and put it back together down here," Georgia said. "I don't see but the one door in or out."

"I'll go in," Penny said, responding to the others' unspoken question.

She might find nothing but darkness and dust inside the temple, but she could also find something that would utterly destroy her. In the back of her mind, she knew she hadn't yet come to grips with having slaughtered most of the town. They'd surely had it coming, but it was all still a sin on a massive scale, wasn't it? Even knowing the gods in the universe cared nothing at all for the human race wasn't enough to take the sting of guilt from what she'd done. Because if there was no gentle afterlife to hope for, then that meant the life here on Earth was the most precious thing of all. If her mind ever fully felt the gravity of the lives she'd snuffed out and the orphans she'd created, she wasn't sure that she'd care to go on living.

So, she would leave her fate to the black temple. She'd fight for her life, but if she wasn't strong enough to fend off whatever lurked inside, she'd take death as her due.

"Just...don't leave me down here, okay?" Penny added. "Wait for me to come back."

They nodded and gave her a flashlight and a crowbar. She walked up the steps, took a deep breath, and pulled open the heavy metal door. Her flashlight illuminated nothing but unadorned black walls inside the temple, but then something gold shone bright in the beam: another of the strange symbols, this one on the far wall.

Penny stepped inside, gripping the crowbar in case something came flying out at her from the darkness.

The floor beneath her gave way. She shrieked as she tumbled down a stone chute, first in darkness, and then in a blue, indistinct twilight—

—she fell onto her hands and knees on a hillside. Instead of grass, she'd landed on a thick mat of gray lichens.

"Clumsy!" her mother exclaimed.

Penny looked up into the strange woman's face and felt herself smile in recognition. "Sorry, Mama!"

Her mother helped her to her feet and they dusted the gray flecks of lichen off her clothes. These hands were not hers, nor the body. Inside this strange new self, Penny reeled. Everything was weird; the air had an unhealthy fungous taint to it, and in the sky—the sky!—there hung a trio of strange, misshapen moons, and opposite the setting sun three black stars rose, their bright coronas gleaming through the streaked clouds.

"Come, Cupra, we better hurry," her mother said. "Your father will be home soon."

The girl took the strange mother's hand and stepped back onto the rocky path toward home. Her old life as Penny and the horrors of Fensmere were rapidly fading away in her mind as if it had all been naught but a daydream; *this* is where she belonged, here in Carcosa with her loving mother and father. She remembered her childhood upon the moors and playing along the shore of the cloudy sea, of going out with her mother to pick herbs and fungus for food and dyeing cloth. Their baskets were full of the most precious mushrooms that produced the royal yellow dye, the colors of the mysterious King and his court, and woe would befall them should any of the nobles be displeased with their craft.

Cupra had heard tales of the King; the whole of Carcosa feared him. She'd seen his minions at the market in town and they were gaunt men and women with faraway stares, quick to anger and quicker to kill. Her parents told her that they were gentle as the spring wind compared to the King himself, and none could so much as look upon the King and maintain their sanity. Cupra had nightmares of the King sometimes, but when she was awake, a tiny part of her thought it must be very exciting to be one of the few who had seen him and lived to tell the tale.

It was nearly dark when she and her mother reached their hut upon the moors. Cupra got to work sorting the lichens and mushrooms onto their drying tables behind the fireplace, and her mother started chopping root vegetables for a stew.

The door banged open. "Ho! Where's my girl?"

"Papa!" Cupra sprang up from her workbench and ran to embrace her father. He caught her in a mighty bear hug, lifted her off her feet and swung her around as if she were a small child. His great red beard tickled her forehead.

The tiny part of her that was still Penny basked in the love like a seedling feeling sunlight for the first time. There in the cozy hut with the lovely smells of her mother's cooking, wrapped in the strong warmth of her father's arms, she was the happiest she had ever been in her life. In that perfect moment, it was as if a door inside her soul had been opened, a door that led to the best possible person she could be. She felt a joy as pure as gold and heady as whiskey.

But then she felt a chill, and there came a slow, thunderous knock at the door.

Her father set her down and quietly shooed her over to her mother's side.

"Who's there?" he called, gripping his hatchet.

The door blew open on a gust of icy air, and there stood the King in his scalloped tatters. A pallid mask obscured his features.

"It is I," the dread King replied in a voice that made Cupra want to tear her ears from her skull. "I have come for new fabric."

"It—it's not ready yet, my liege," her mother said, her voice trembling.

"That is...unfortunate." The King made the barest motion of his hand, and her mother's and father's heads split right down their middles as if they'd been cleaved with invisible mattocks. They fell where they stood, their dark blood spilling across the tidy floorboards.

Cupra wanted to scream, wanted to run, but she found herself rooted to the spot, unable to utter anything but a faint strangled noise.

The King moved toward her, so smoothly it seemed he floated like a ghost. "It's a dangerous thing to fall into the path of a living god, but then you'd know that, wouldn't you, little changeling? Little dimension-hopper. Little murderess."

"Why?" she managed to gasp, staring down at the bodies of her parents.

"Your Lord works in mysterious ways." He took off the pallid mask, and she recoiled from the monstrosity she saw beneath it. But the worst was his eyes: they were the same terrifying black as the dark stars she'd seen upon the horizon.

He leaned down and gave her a kiss, and suddenly that dreadful darkness was flowing into her mouth, down her throat, filling her very core, and she knew this was a living curse.

She stumbled back, retched, but the darkness would not leave her, and when she looked up again, the King was gone, and she was alone with her slaughtered parents.

Her world destroyed, Cupra fled. Where could she go? Her mother's sister lived in Carcosa City. Perhaps she would take mercy on her. The girl ran two miles to the city of tall towers, but the guards at the wall barred her entrance.

"You bear the curse of the King, and you may not enter," the first guard told her, solid and immoveable as a stone in his gray uniform.

"But he killed my parents; where can I go?" she pleaded.

"Go find someone who could love the likes of you," the second guard said. "But that is surely not here."

Despondent, Cupra turned away from the city gate, but a beggar in grimy rags called out, "Hoy, girl!"

Cupra approached the beggar. "Yes?"

"Lost your parents, did you?" His tone was sympathetic.

Cupra nodded, heartbroken.

"Go to the kingdom of the South. The King and Queen there are known to love all who enter their realm."

And so Cupra walked for days and weeks, living off what edible lichens she could find, drinking what dew she could collect in leaf-funnels overnight. The darkness inside her was as heavy as a mountain; she felt she was always a moment away from tears, but as time wore on it became harder and harder to cry. Sometimes, she'd come to a town and try to find a doorway to sleep in or a scrap of discarded bread, but a guard would always find her and chase her outside the city limits.

She was but skin and bones when she reached the border of the Southern kingdom. As she crested the hill outside the kingdom's gates, her eyes widened as she beheld the line of ragged people on the red carpet that stretched across the barren valley below her, all waiting to be admitted to the green meadows and fruit-heavy orchards beyond the gates.

Cupra climbed down the hill and took a spot at the back of the line, half expecting the people around her to start pointing at her and shout her away back into the wilderness, but nobody did. The others were just as thin and ragged as she, just as travel-weary, just as desperate. They couldn't see past their own miseries long enough to realize that she'd been cursed.

The line moved forward, but it soon seemed people were just pressing up against the front gates rather than moving through. The crush of bodies made her nervous, made her think about abandoning the line entirely, but she heard beastly howling and realized that someone had released huge dire wolves that were pacing just beyond the red carpet, eyeing the people hungrily. Each monstrous canid wore a red, brass-spiked collar decorated with the royal crest of the Southern kingdom.

"Prospective citizens!" called a woman, her voice floating like music over the crowd.

Cupra looked up, and her breath caught in her throat. Atop the kingdom gates stood a man and a woman dressed in silver and silken sky blue robes, and they were both the most beautiful people she had ever seen. In that moment, Cupra had hope that if she could just be in the same room as the King and Queen of the South, she might find her happiness again, and the curse of the King in Yellow might be lifted.

"We are honored that so many of you wish to join our kingdom," the handsome king said.

"We are a kingdom of love, and once you step through our gates, you shall need nothing else!" the beautiful queen declared. "You will never be hungry or thirsty again, because you shall not need food in our land, only our love."

"Therefore, to prepare yourself, we ask only that you remove that which you shall not need."

Two soldiers carrying large leather sacks began traveling down the line handing something out to each person in the line. Cupra wondered what it could be until a soldier pressed the handle of a very sharp knife into her hand. She stared down at the shining blade, wondering dumbly what she was supposed to do with it.

"Do you love us?" asked the queen.

"We love you!" cried the crowd.

"Do you want our love?" asked the king.

"Yes!" the starving people moaned.

"Then hollow yourselves," the queen ordered. "Be rid of your distasteful entrails. Hollow yourselves, and we shall fill you with our love."

A man near the front of the line screamed.

Another cried out, "Ah, it hurts, my queen!"

"If your love for us is true, you will be strong, and you will survive! Only those whose love is false and weak shall fall and be fed to the wolves."

Shrieks and wails rose all around Cupra as the desperate people began to hollow themselves in hopes of gaining the love of the beautiful king and queen. The darkness inside her ached like molten lead as she stared down at the knife blade. All around her, people fell to the rocky ground outside the red carpet—now, finally, she knew why it was red—and she could hear the snarling and rending of bone and flesh as the dire wolves put those who hadn't quite managed to hollow themselves out of their misery.

"Girl."

She looked up, and a blue uniformed soldier upon a dappled gray warhorse loomed above her. He pointed his crossbow at her. "Don't you feel the love?"

"Yes," she replied. "I do feel it."

Cupra plunged the blade into her belly, and the darkness spewed forth from her wound, the darkness of a million poisoned stars, and it flooded the whole landscape, sweeping away the soldiers and wolves and miserable people. The gorgeous king and queen screamed and tried for higher ground but there was none to be found, and they, too, were swept away in the black ocean.

Finally, the darkness receded, and Cupra stood alone in the wasteland, mutely clutching her wound.

Alone but for the King in Yellow at her side.

"Well done, my child," he said. "Carcosa has but one King, and I shall stand for no others."

He paused. "Tell me, child. You came here as your last hope, and you found nothing but death. Is your spirit broken? Have you lost all faith?"

"Yes," she whispered.

"Good," he replied. "Then I have one last task for you. I've been to that planet of yours, and I think I'd like it best if the only sounds were the wind in the dead trees and the waves crashing upon empty shores."

He gave her a shove. The ground opened beneath her and she tumbled into a great dark chasm—

—Penny landed hard on her back inside the temple, trying to pull the crablike creature off her face.

Just relax and open your mouth, it whispered inside her mind. *Be a good girl and it'll all be over soon.*

Keeping her mouth clamped shut, Penny struggled to the bronze door and kicked it open.

"Oh, sweet Jesus!" she heard Jay exclaim.

"Don't just stand there; help her!" Georgia shot back.

The others finally pried the creature off her, and they beat it to death on the concrete with crowbars and baseball bats while Penny coughed and gasped for breath.

"Miss Penny, are you all right?" Georgia asked after it was clear the creature was dead.

She nodded, rubbing her throat.

"What do you reckon you want to do now?" Bessie asked.

"We can't ever let anyone go in there ever again." Penny nodded toward the basalt temple.

"Should we get some bars to put across the door?" Georgia asked.

"We should burn it," Penny told the women who had labored in the mansion for years in near slavery. "Burn down the whole place to the ground and if it leaves a hole we fill it with concrete."

"Why, bless your heart," Georgia replied. "I believe it would be my pleasure to do that very thing."

Jessie Shimmer Goes to Hell

I raised my Mossberg shotgun and trained it on the front door of the old shack. My hands were quivering; I tried to steady them. If Miko was still in full possession of her powers, the shotgun might as well have been a water pistol, but maybe the parasitic Goad inside her had weakened her. That same devil had once possessed me; she had tried to take my soul but got it instead. A lucky break for me, but it made the afterlives of the thousands of other souls trapped inside her horrifyingly worse. I couldn't leave them all to suffer like that. I just couldn't.

"Miko, are you in there?" I shouted far louder than necessary, but I was trying to get myself fired up so that maybe I wouldn't feel so damn scared. "We can help each other, Miko…you want that devil out of you, don't you? I can help you with that."

No reply.

I inhaled deeply through my nose, and began to step carefully onto the creaking porch, watching the dark windows. Seeing no movement, no sign of ambush, I pushed the empty screen frame aside with my boot and nudged the front door open with the barrel of my shotgun.

"Miko?" I whispered.

In the dimness, I saw the dusty frame of an old Army surplus cot, the olive drab fabric rotted to tatters, and a couple of broken-down lawn chairs decorated with a scattering of crushed beer cans. An old Marlboro ashtray and a discarded bait bucket lay amongst the blown-in leaves on the warped, dirty floor. Faded posters of dogs playing poker and some forgotten Playboy Playmate decorated the far wall. Nothing moved. I held my breath, listening for sounds of boards creaking under shifting feet, sounds of someone else's breathing, but all I could hear was my own pulse pounding in my ears.

I pushed the door open a little wider and stepped inside.

A sudden blur of movement from the shadows, and something grabbed the barrel of the shotgun, yanking me into the shack, jerking my finger on the shotgun's trigger. The boom nearly deafened me. Miko gave a grunt of pain and released the gun, but she'd already sent me tumbling sideways. I caught a glimpse of her belly torn wide open by the shotgun blast as I went past her. I fell heavily and slid across the gritty floor. My impact knocked one of the lawn chairs over and sent beer cans clattering, but I didn't lose my grip on my shotgun.

I barely had time to sit up and rack another cartridge into the chamber before she'd gathered her slippery guts up and expertly packed them back into her body, her flesh sealing below her fingers. I'd never seen any creature be able to heal itself so quickly, not even a werewolf in full lunacy.

"Miko, I can help—" I began, but she screamed and leaped at me, the movement inhumanly fast.

So much for negotiation, I thought as I swung my shotgun up, managing to catch her hard under her chin with the barrel as she fell upon me. I pulled the trigger. The blast took the left half of her head off, showering me with blood and bits of bone and brains. Snapshot memories of thousands of deaths flashed through my mind in quick succession. I was momentarily dazzled, but they weren't strong enough to pull me in.

And…she wasn't stopping. My horror turned to the most abject, shivering terror I've ever felt. Making a terrible gargling noise, she swung at me with her left fist as she wrestled me for the shotgun with her right. I ducked her first punch, but her second connected with my right eye with a nasty bone crack and my vision went white with pain.

In that precious second of lost consciousness, I'd let go of my weapon and had gone sprawling on my back. Miko stood over me, holding my shotgun by the barrel, glaring down at me with her one good eye as her blasted-apart head dripped blood down her naked body. Most of her brains had slithered out of the wet red cavity of her skull and right then I realized that flesh was nothing more than a convenient vessel for whatever she had become. Her own body was as much a meat puppet as those of any of the townspeople she'd possessed. And in her green glare, she promised me unimaginable torment.

My mind raced like a rabbit from one desperate idea to another. Gouge out her remaining eye? No guarantee that would actually take away her sight. Try to blast her with incendiary ectoplasm? I'd burn myself just as badly as I'd burn her. And what could burning do to her, anyhow? She was about to carve me up like a holiday turkey and she didn't even have a working nervous system.

So I slapped my hand on her gory ankle, closed my eyes and willed us both into my private hell. I'd tried to make the hellement homier by turning it into a recreation of my old bedroom back home. The décor change almost made up for the bad vibes from the endless stock of bad memories I'd stored in there. Almost.

Miko shoved me hard, sending me tumbling over the bed and into my dresser.

"*Korosu-zo!* How dare you do this to me?" she screamed. Her head and body were whole again but she was opening her mouth so wide her skull was deforming. She didn't seem quite real here in my hellement; she looked more like one of those creepy silicone sex dolls you can buy for a couple thousand bucks off the Internet. All the parts for supernatural hotness were still there, but they didn't add up to the hormone-enslaving whole she wielded in the living world.

Not that she was the least bit interested in seducing me or anyone else at that moment.

"I can help." I inched toward the enchanted sword and shield I kept in the corner.

"Fuck your help." Miko stepped forward, then winced, shuddering, holding her head and doubling over as if she'd been hit with a sudden migraine. My devil was probably rocking her inner world. I took the opportunity to grab my defenses, slinging my shield onto my left arm.

"I'm serious." I gripped my sword and pointed it at her, but made no move to attack. "I can help you."

My weapon-hand was steady. Being in my own domain had calmed my fears considerably, and now I was focused on my goal: getting the stolen souls out of her safely. If I could destroy her after that, great, but killing her before I'd tried to rescue the innocents inside her was no good at all. And I wasn't even remotely sure that she was killable, anyhow. I blinked my magic stone eye through to the view that had once shown me a shadow-devil's vulnerable heart in my boyfriend's hell. But I saw nothing inside Miko's doll body, just a solid darkness.

Maybe if I fought her hard enough, she'd have second thoughts about laying waste to another isolated town. If I could prevent her from staging another mass murder, that would be almost as good as taking her out of commission entirely, wouldn't it? A smaller victory, sure, but it would still be a victory.

"We can help each other," I repeated.

She straightened up, slowly, giving me a look that was pure death. "I don't need help."

"Sure you do," I said reasonably. "It's my devil, and I know how to kill it. I can take it right out of you. And I'm thinking that if *you* knew how to get rid of it on your own, you'd have done it by now, right?"

Boy, did that piss her off. Miko snarled and launched herself at me, and I jumped back, right into the dresser. The mirror rattled against the wall. The room was way too small to fight her. In an instant I willed away the entire building and we were in the middle of the broad, spacious lawn where my parents' house would have been in my old neighborhood.

I sidestepped her lunge and gave her a solid thwack with my shield, sending her tumbling across the grass. But she wasn't down long. She flipped herself over fast as a cat and leaped at me again. I raised my shield to deal her a second blow, but her move was a feint and she punched the tendon bundle on the inside of my right wrist, knocking my sword out of my hand and leaving my whole arm tingling.

She darted after the enchanted sword, snatching it up from the lush grass with her left hand. But the sword didn't want to be held, at least not by her. Miko's palm and fingers sizzled on the leather grip. She didn't let go of the burning weapon and merely smiled at me through clenched white teeth.

"I learned to master pain a long time ago," she said. "Let's see how you do with it once I've rammed this down your pretty throat."

She raised the sword toward me, her left hand smoking horribly now, and I realized her switchblade had appeared in her right hand. Oh, crap. How did she do that? She gave the stiletto a casual twirl over the backs of her fingers and into her fist again, like a professional gambler turning a table trick with a poker chip.

I raised my shield and began to back up, trying to think of a new strategy. Once she made her next attack, I could defend against the sword, but she'd slice me to ribbons with her stiletto before I could say "sashimi." I'd been hurt in here before, hurt badly, but not mortally. What would happen if she cut my throat, tore out my heart? Would I die? Could she take my soul? Or would my soul be trapped in here forever, my body another puppet for her to use as she pleased? I shuddered to think of the twisted games she would play with my boyfriend once she had control of my flesh and could pretend to be me.

The portal door was just a few feet away. I could make a run for it—but what then? She'd manifested her switchblade; if she had more time in here by herself, would she start figuring out ways of taking over my hellement? My gut told me the answer was a resounding "yes" and she'd do it a lot more quickly than the shadow-devil had. Would she figure a way out and start possessing my body as the Goad had? Jesus. The danger was too great. I couldn't possibly run; I had to find some way to subdue her.

I knew the jarred traumas I'd stored in my hellement were just a few feet behind me. She might have a tremendous tolerance for physical pain, but she didn't really seem to like it much, either. And what about emotional pain?

Miko lunged at me again, and I braced myself, trying to make my body small behind the shield. She was almost on me when she gave a gasp and fell to her knees. My Goad was giving me another bit of good luck. I jumped backwards into the jars and grabbed the nearest one; by the feel of it, it was a night of torment at a sadist's cruel hands.

The jar opened with a pop in my shield hand just as Miko recovered and rushed me. I threw the silver liquid right in her eyes. Howling, she dropped her blades and fell onto the grass, writhing in agony, clawing at her face.

I grabbed another jar—the memory of a woman being flayed to death—as Miko frantically tried to scrape away the heavy fluid.

"I'll stop if you agree to my terms," I shouted at her, loud so my voice would carry through whatever she was hearing in the memory.

Miko snarled something unintelligible, maybe it was Japanese and maybe it was just word-salad, but she was getting up again so I threw the contents of the second jar at her, getting more in her mouth this time. She collapsed, retching, twitching in the throes of the re-lived murder.

"You want more? Really?" I loosened the lid on a third jar: a friend getting his throat cut open. I knew *that* one was plenty unpleasant. "I've got hundreds of these. Thousands, maybe. I can do this *forever*. But say the word and I'll stop."

Miko slowly rose to her knees as she wiped her face off, fat silver droplets tumbling down her neck and cleavage, sticking briefly in her pubic hair before they fell into the blades of grass. Then she raised her hands, palms up in a surrendering gesture. I didn't believe it, so I flipped the lid off and kept the jar ready.

"Okay, enough." Her voice was hoarse, and she didn't take her eyes off the memory in my hand. "What do you want?"

"I'll kill the Goad inside you, put it out of your misery. But you have to do something for me in return."

"What?"

"I want you to release the souls you took in Cuchillo."

Her eerie, beautiful features twisted in anger and indignation. "No!"

"Then we have a problem." I cocked my arm back, ready to let the next trauma fly.

She flinched. "Wait! Stop. I…I will let any souls leave me, *if* they want to leave. I won't cast out those that prefer my afterlife."

I frowned at her. "They'll have free will to make the choice? And we'll all be free to go back to the living world, without your interference?"

"Yes, you and they will be free." Grimacing, she wiped the rest of the memories off her face and scrubbed her hands clean on the grass.

I paused, considering. "I don't trust you. I need a binding promise. A blood oath."

Using the sharp nail of her left index finger, she cut an X in the skin above her heart and held her hand over the bleeding cuts. Blood welled between her fingers. "I swear on my own soul that I am standing down to allow Jessie Shimmer into my domain. If she slays the devil plaguing my world, I will allow any souls in my possession to leave with her if they so choose. I will not interfere, and I will allow her and the souls who follow her to re-enter the living world unharmed."

She cleared her throat and looked at me, her expression a mixture of suspicion and disdain. "Does this oath meet with your approval?"

I licked my lips, trying to imagine any loopholes that Miko could use to strangle me. "Promise you won't try to keep me from killing the devil. Promise you won't try to hurt me or my friends when we get back to the living world."

Her fingers tightened over her wound. "I further swear on my own soul that I will in no way hinder Jessie Shimmer while she is in my domain. Nor will I attempt to harm her or anyone else of concern to her when we return to the living world."

She stopped for a moment, staring at me. "However, I do *not* promise I will not harm her or her friends should the opportunity arise after this cursed day is over."

Well, I sure as hell wasn't expecting her to declare us BFFs after everything that had happened. This was probably the best I was going to get out of her. I took a deep breath and nodded. "Okay, then. Let's do this."

After I gathered up the spilled traumas and sealed them back in their jars, I armed myself with my sword and shield and faced Miko, who was still on her knees in the grass.

"Okay, so…how do I enter your domain from here?" I asked.

"Easily enough."

She put her hands at the base of her neck, right over the indentation where her sternum met her collarbones, and dug her fingers in. Blood spilled as her skin tore, and she quickly worked her nails across her clavicle, then down her sternum, down between her breasts, down her taut belly. As she tore herself open and pulled her skin away, she revealed not red muscle and bone but that utter blackness I'd seen before with my stone eye.

"Step inside." She held her flayed skin wide as if it were merely a coat, and a gust of bitter wind blew from her core, as if it led to some ancient, frozen depth on a planet so far away from any sun that not so much as a rumor of light ever reached it. The blood dripping down the ragged edges of her skin steamed, froze.

I stared at the icy void within her, feeling my stomach churn. But this was nothing more than what I'd bargained for. There was no turning back now. There was no way out but to keep going through with the plan.

"All right." I took a deep breath, held my sword and shield close, and jumped down inside Miko's hell.

First came the spinning disorientation and blindness I'd come to expect, but it was cold, so cold, and my eyes and lungs were burning as if I were floating unprotected in deep space, and I felt as though I might be torn apart, when—

—a sensation like falling onto rotten pond ice, plunging down into dark frigid water. I gripped my sword and shield tightly; I couldn't lose my grip on my only protection here—

I lay in the slagged wreckage, small and weak, my infant voice wailing in pain for the mother who'd expelled me from her rotting womb and abandoned me. The metal and brick and charred bones around me were hot with radiation, my flesh burning and healing over and over, the hunger in me far brighter than the sun trying to force its rays through the smoke-dark skies—

No, no, that wasn't me, that wasn't my memory. I reached to wipe silver trauma from my face with my shield hand, but I felt no liquid metal, just the dark water I was drowning in. Thrashing for air, I found the cold jagged edge of the ice above me. I swung my sword hand skyward, my weapon still clenched in my shivering fist, and hauled myself up into harsh air. Both my eyes almost immediately froze shut. Gasping from the cold, I started to crawl across the rough ice toward what I hoped was shore when I felt the surface begin to give way beneath me—

I could smell the little boy in the crib crammed next to mine. The wet nurse had given me a bottle of watered-down milk, but it soured in my stomach and I spit it all up. I felt so hungry and empty, but none of the exhausted orphanage staff paid any attention to our wails after the lights were out.

I didn't know what I yearned for, except that I wanted to be near that little boy who was so warm and smelled so good. My infant bones were still rubbery, my muscles weak, but after a few tries I managed to stand, grasp the wooden crib rail, and pull myself up and over into his bed—

No. Not that. I didn't want to feel what was coming next. I shook myself out of Miko's memory and hauled myself back onto the ice.

It crazed and crackled beneath me as I scrambled toward the rocky dam, but I reached the glazed stones and managed to throw myself onto them before the pond-top shattered. I lay there, clinging to the rocks, gasping for breath, the frigid air like a thousand needles in my lungs. My water-stringy hair was freezing into icicle dreadlocks, and I could see frost crystals spreading across the sleeve of my jacket. To top it all off, my eyelids froze over my damn ocularis again.

It's not really cold in here, I told myself. *It's not really* anything *in here. This is all the Goad's illusion. See through it.*

My pep talk wasn't working, not even a little bit, and I could feel the knees of my leather pants freezing to the stones beneath me. I started crawling forward toward the bank, still gripping my shield and weapon. My gloves were turning hard as iron, but at least they were keeping the rocks from skinning my knuckles. The land surrounding the pond was a huge, beautifully landscaped garden that had suffered a fierce ice storm; tulips and roses were bent nearly double, their ice-sheathed heads touching the ground. The limbs of flowering bushes and small cherry trees were also burdened, dragging low, twigs and branches threatening to break at any moment.

I collapsed again as I reached solid ground. The pavestones below me felt as though they were sucking every last joule of heat from my core. I wasn't sure what it would be like to freeze to death, whether it would hurt as tiny razors of ice seeded in my flesh and sliced open my cells, or if it would simply be a numb drifting-away, but I was pretty sure I was within just a few minutes of finding that out.

In my boyfriend's hell, when I'd switched to a different ocularis view, my entire perception of the dimension had changed, not just my vision. Roughly the same things were happening, but the people were different, the scenery had changed, even the air was different. Could it work here, too? I prayed that it would.

My whole body was shivering and my flesh was so numb I could barely feel any of what I was doing. I cracked the ice sealing leather to leather and slipped my leaden arm out of the straps so I could set my shield down on the stones. With effort, I got to my knees and sat in the padded concave interior. I dared not let go of my sword, and I dared not let my shield get far from me. For all I knew, the Goad was lurking just out of sight, waiting to snatch away my protection.

I dearly wished I could summon my fire to my left hand. Seeing Miko bring her switchblade into my hellement made me wonder if it was possible, but sitting there with the freeze seeping into my brain I couldn't figure the trick out. I pressed the chilly palm of my left hand to the eyelids frozen over my cold ocularis, hoping it would warm, willing it to warm.

Finally, *finally*, the frost melted and my torpid eye muscles started working again, and I was able to blink. Once. Nothing. Twice. Nothing. Thrice. Nothing.

Not a goddamned thing. I couldn't see *anything* through my ocularis. Had the cold broken it?

Oh God, oh God, c'mon, I'm dying here. I took a deep, lung-torturing breath and blinked again.

The garden around me changed, and I felt warmth flow back into my body. What had been trees and bushes and flowerbeds I now saw were people—tens of thousands of people—standing, crouching, lying on the ground. They were all immobilized in glassy chrysalises, their souls red and orange and purple lights burning within, tiny factories generating energy for the devil who'd trapped them. I could see the expressions of the dozen closest to me; they weren't having pleasant dreams inside their prisons.

Okay, then. I quietly moved off my shield and slung it back on my arm, staring past the souls into the darkness between them, trying to see what might lie there. When Miko had tried to take my soul, she'd mistakenly absorbed the one surviving larval Goad that had still been lurking in my hellement. What did the little devil look like now? Its mother was a vast, flaccid creature in my boyfriend's hell, a genuine monster that had grown fat on decades of angst, forcing her prey to relive their personal horrors over and over. But her child had only been in Miko's hell for a couple of days. It hadn't had much time to mature to an adult form, but it had over a thousand times more souls to feed from.

So was the young Goad still a small, quick spongelike larva? Or had it gotten huge and sedentary like its mother? I kept creeping along the path, watching the dark places for movement.

And then as I was scanning a small rocky hill…the whole thing shifted and undulated toward me. I felt the hair rise on the back of my neck. Crap. My stone eye focused more closely on the "hill", and I saw it was pocked with hollows and burrows. In some holes, I saw fluttering tentacles I knew it used to taste and smell. In others, I saw circular grinding orifices like the toothy maws of hagfish. And in others shone glossy, deep-black eyes the size of basketballs.

A few days feeding off tens of thousands of souls' agonies had sped its growth beyond anything I'd imagined. It wasn't as huge as its momma, but it could still move around, and that made it more dangerous. At least it either wasn't old enough or big enough to spawn yet. I watched its black eyes, and realized that (of course) they were starting to focus on me.

Great. Just great.

I sidestepped to the nearest trapped soul. She was curled like a fetus within her prison, naked. Her features were blurred, distorted further by her agonized expression. She looked to be maybe 18 or 19. Could she be awakened? I rapped on her chrysalis. The glassy surface was granite-solid, unyielding. I hit it again, harder, and she inside stirred and moaned, but did not open her eyes.

"Hey, wake up!" I called to her, sounding stupidly desperate even to myself. She was a stranger; if I knew anything about her, knew her name at the very least, *maybe* I could pull her out of the trauma she was re-living. But otherwise? I might as well have tried to awaken a marble statue.

The mountainous Goad made another ground-shaking lurch in my direction. Was it genuinely slow or just trying to trick me into thinking it was too heavy to fly? Its mother was only able to work the illusions of the hell to try to trap me, relying on her swarming children for protection. While most of the brood had been as bright as angry hornets, this particular offspring had already proved it was fairly clever.

I looked around at the trapped souls again, trying to think of a workable attack plan as I searched for anyone familiar. But none of the souls near me were recognizable through their chrysalis blurs. I'd only talked to a few of the townsfolk before they fell to Miko. How could I find any of them in here amongst these thousands? And what good could one or two of them do even if I somehow freed them before the Goad devoured me or did any of a thousand other horrible things that dangled from the gallows of my imagination?

The Goad made a low rumbling noise. "I sssseeee you, mongrellll."

Well, it knew about as much English as its mother. I met its dark, hundred-eyed gaze, raising my sword and shield. "Great. You see me. What now?"

"Now you run!"

The Goad flattened itself, its spongy blob of a body rippling, and then it released, springing high into the air, sailing fast toward me, fifty tons of oily, ink-black flesh ready to squash me like a blueberry under a rancid side of beef.

Christ on a cracker. Yeah, I ran. Fast as I could, and I'd barely cleared its crush zone when I heard and felt it slamming down to the ground right behind me. I felt a moment of relief, slowed a little and chanced a glance backward.

Black tentacles were shooting out of the sides of the Goad like cannon-fired harpoons from a pirate ship. I tried to run faster, but a tentacle whipped into the back of my thigh, knocking me down. I tried to get some purchase on the damp grass to crawl away but the tentacle slithered tight around my leg and began to drag me back toward the monster.

I swore and managed to flip myself over as it hauled me across the damp ground, reeling me in like a sport fish. One of those horrible grinding mouths spasmed just above the pore the tentacle was retreating into. Snack time, and I was the chef's special. I tucked my shield close to my body and held my sword ready.

Only seconds left before the tentacle would yank me into the Goad's maw. I would have only one chance at this. My shield was maybe a little bigger than the circumference of the mouth, maybe—

—a sudden jerk and I was there, the tentacle whipping me up at that looming garbage disposal orifice. I rammed the shield against the undulating teeth. As the mouth twitched, scraping the metal, seeming unsure of what to do with this unexpected resistance, I drove the point of my sword deep into the oily, gritty flesh. Dark ichor that stank of diesel spurted from the wound. It was like cutting into oilfield mud. I carved my blade down hard in an arc around the outer lip of the mouth, trying to sever the muscles controlling the grinding jaws.

It was working. I felt part of the mouth go slack, but tentacles grabbed both my booted feet, pulling them in opposite directions like I was a wishbone the monster wanted to snap. I jerked my blade free from the sucking flesh and slashed the tentacles constricting my feet. They were tough as tire rubber, but I hacked them away.

The Goad was shuddering, shifting, corpulent muscles bunching beneath its foul skin. It was going to try for another jump. Or maybe it was just going to flop over. Either way, it would crush me. I had to find its heart, had to kill it as quickly as possible before it could do the same to me.

I slipped my arm out of the shield still jamming its mouth, took a rib-straining breath, shut my eyes, then plunged into the cut I'd made, slicing deeper with my sword while I tore at the greasy flesh with my left hand and the toes of my boots. The monster's inner tissues had a loose, pulpy feel, like the inside of a huge citrus fruit, as if it had been growing so quickly that its meat hadn't had a chance to fill in and harden. But that lax texture made my task easier. I burrowed into its body, ignoring the stinging ichor, relying on touch and my instincts to tell me how far to go.

The beast roared and writhed. The flesh around me contracted as if it were trying to push me out. But after everything the Goad had done to me, after it had turned me into a cannibal, infected me, tried to kill me, I wasn't about to stop. Oh hell no. And I was close. I could feel the pulse and heat of its heart, see the red glow of it even through my closed eyelids.

I plunged my left hand through the last membrane into the burning magma auricle, connecting myself to the source of its diabolic power, and the current ran through me, a dark electricity that lit up my every synapse and nerve ending with sparks and shadows of the trapped multitudes' personal torments. My hand was in flaming agony, but I knew I could bear it. I had been through worse. The Goad's roar turned to a terrified shriek as I pulled its vile life energy into the reservoir in my hellement.

The beast shuddered in seizures, and its flesh began to fall apart from the inside out, a rotting house of loose meat. The current disconnected as the devil died, and I fell back amongst the oily charnel rubble, gasping for air, spitting out the Goad's foul fluids, wiping my eyes clear on my sleeves. My left hand was a barbecued mess, but I was too high on adrenaline to feel much pain.

It was the most disgusting thing I'd ever done, but I was overjoyed: I'd won. And now Miko had to hold up her end of our bargain. Grinning, I began kicking through the stink to find my shield.

Fable Fusion

A tale of the 7th Doctor and his companion Ace; originally appeared in *Doctor Who Short Trips: Destination Prague*

Cowritten with Gary A. Braunbeck

The little girl knelt at the edge of the pit in the great stone floor, her unwashed hair obscuring her face. The dress she wore was old and tattered, but Ace could see that the garment had been cared for with the greatest affection and tenderness. The girl remained quite still, as if waiting for something important, something glorious, something that was, at the very least, well…*fun*.

She did not have to wait long.

From the depths of the pit came the sound of a violin; softly at first, but with a great, determined pulse in the lower register. Its slowness imbued it with tremendous purpose, like a dance-hall comic telling a complex shaggy-dog story as he worked his way toward the corker of a punchline. The sound immediately relaxed the little girl's body as she whispered: "Oh, Papa, this is going to be a good'un, isn't it?"

The note rose in pitch and intensity, releasing a single, sustained note that hung in the air, unwavering, until finally it pierced through her, creating a feeling of such sweetness, such delight, such unbound giddiness, that her body trembled from the pure, unapologetic *hilarity* of the note; it wrapped itself around her like a fine, delicate thread, over and over, cocooning her in its eloquent and sharp wit, and the girl—as if being tickled by dozen of fingers—fell on her side giggling and waving her hands.

"Oh, Papa, that's the funniest one yet!"

No sooner had the spell been cast than it was broken by a sound from outside the castle; the loud, rough, grinding, metallic grunting sound—*vworp-vworp-vworp!*—of some machine trying to come to life or die quickly.

From deep in the pit, the music of the violin stopped. The little girl snapped up her head, tossing the hair from her face, and gazed in the direction of the ugly mechanical sound with a blazing, unbound anger bordering on hatred.

Ace felt as if the little girl were focusing that hatred directly at her, and jolted out of her nap in a damp sweat.

"Ace," called the Doctor's voice from elsewhere in the TARDIS. "Best prepare yourself, dear girl. Upsy-lazy. We'll be arriving shortly."

Shaking off the remnants of the odd little dream, Ace threw back the covers and ran toward the shower, dropping her clothes along the way as if they were breadcrumbs carefully scattered in a forest to help her find her way home.

Ace had just finished drying her hair when she felt the TARDIS change direction and begin to descend. She slipped on a fluffy patchwork robe and stuck her head into the control room. The Doctor was bent over the controls, scowling in thought.

"Hey, Professor, I had the weirdest dream while I was—hey, what's this? I thought we were going to Risa for a bit of a vacation. I could use some tropical surroundings after being cooped up in here—nothing personal."

"Bit of a change in plans, I'm afraid—and no offense taken," The Doctor replied. "I've gotten an encrypted transdimensional call for help. Audio only, no video."

"From Gallifrey?" Ace asked.

The Doctor made a face. "Oh, heavens no, not that lot. This appears to be generated by the backup emergency call system I set up for U.N.I.T. But the time and place are wrong—it sounds like Elizabeth Shaw of all people, but it's coming from Prague in May of 2050."

"Who's Elizabeth Shaw?" asked Ace.

The Doctor gave her a quick smile. "One of the brightest scientific minds of her generation, but I'm afraid I quite supplanted her in the eyes of the Brigadier when I joined U.N.I.T. Gave her a bit of a hard time, I expect."

Ace smiled. "You? *Never.*"

The Doctor gave her a sharp look. "At any rate, she'd be...well, she'd be quite elderly in 2050. And this was the voice of a young woman."

"So maybe she traveled in time, or found the Fountain of Youth," Ace replied. "Or maybe someone's stolen the emergency communicator."

"All are indeed possibilities," he replied. "But as I cannot resist a damsel in distress, we're going down to investigate. Put on your walking boots, Ace...but leave the Nitro-9 behind, all right?"

"Aw, Professor!"

"The situation down there might be explosive enough without your well-intended chemical contribution. Should the need arise, I'll let you return to supply our defensive needs."

"All right." She felt naked without her nitro.

"Look on the bright side, Ace. Prague is a lovely and fascinating city even in the ugliest of its eras, and always full of surprises. Consider, if you will, a few high points of its illustrious history. The city was saved from the ravages of WWII and the Third Reich because of its beauty; it is home to Rabi Loew's mythic 'Golem', Rudolph II's obsession with finding the elixir of youth, the scientific genius in the form of Kepler and Tycho Brahe, and the alchemical obsessions of Magister Kelly." He slapped together his hands and began rubbing them furiously. "Oh, the wonders of the place."

"Never been before, myself," she replied. "That whole iron curtain thing rather put a damper on going there for holiday when I was growing up."

"Quite so, quite so. Well, let us hope the geopolitical climate is much improved since those dark days."

He slapped the well-worn Panama hat on his head. "Do I look presentable?"

Ace titled her head to the side and grinned. "Did anyone ever tell you, Professor, that in that get-up you insist on wearing, you look just like a dance-hall comic?"

The Doctor raised his eyebrows, hooked his thumbs through his suspenders, and bounced on the balls of his feet. "Well, if I do say so myself, I *have* been known to elocute a ripping yarn or two in my day. I'm not without my share of mirth and joviality, despite what you may think, my dear Ace. I can be quite the funny fellow."

She smiled. "A regular *Monty Python* player you are, I fancy."

The Doctor stopped bouncing, looking as if his pride had been wounded slightly. "We haven't the time for me to display the full depth and breadth of my redoubtable wit, Ace. Get dressed; I expect that we'll have some investigating to do today. The usual mysteries and enigmas and conundrums which none but us can unravel." He paused for a moment, then added: "Dear me, I do hope we're not falling into a rut."

Ace opted for a stretchy pair of black jeans and some well-worn Doc Martens she'd picked up in a late-90s boutique in Chicago. It took her just a few minutes to dress, brush out her damp hair and secure it in a ponytail.

She felt the TARDIS materialize and set down with a slight thump just as she emerged from her room.

The Doctor stood by the front door, twirling his umbrella. "Let's see what there is to see, shall we?"

Ace slipped on her black jacket, slung her battered rucksack over her shoulder, and followed the Doctor out into what seemed to be the best-outfitted laboratory she'd ever seen.

"*Wicked*," she whispered. The building was an old church, and sunlight through the myriad stained-glass windows shone down on a room full of gleaming white lab tables, computers, and delicate glass experimental setups. A half-dozen university-aged researchers in white lab coats were staring openmouthed at The Doctor, Ace, and the TARDIS.

"Wicked indeed," said the Doctor, then muttered, darkly: "I sense that something's very wrong here."

"What, them?" Ace asked, nodding toward the lab workers. "They look all right to me."

"No, not them, silly." He waved the crooked, question-mark-shaped end of his umbrella at the others and called, "Hello there! Sorry to drop in like this! Please, don't mind us. Carry on, carry on."

An auburn-haired woman in a white lab coat stood up from behind a computer and smiled. "You *must* be The Doctor."

He doffed his hat and took a bow. "Indeed I am, in the flesh, as it were. And you are?"

"I'm Dr. Elizabeth Holub. I'm the principal investigator for this lab. You knew my grandmother, Elizabeth Shaw. She once told me that should anything go seriously wrong, something beyond anything I'd seen before, I should contact you. I apologize if my doing so was presumptuous, but...I've simply run out of ideas."

"What's happening here?" The Doctor asked, gesturing at the activity in the massive lab.

"The main goal here is to develop a new type of cold fusion, much colder and cheaper than the type they worked out at UCLA a few years ago. Regular people can't afford petrol or even firewood any more—you undoubtedly know of the bloodshed caused by the petrol riots that have been going on for some time now. The new hydrogen cells have been fiddly and are still quite expensive. People need better options for generating electricity for their households."

"Indeed," The Doctor replied. "A most admirable goal. How's it been going?"

"Six months ago we achieved stable fusion at 100°C—no hotter than boiling water. When the process goes beyond those parameters it simply fails with an exceedingly low chance of explosion. We sent the process out to select labs for further experiments and confirmation, and so far they've all reported that our technique works wonderfully for them.

"The problem," Elizabeth continued, "is that over the past month it's gradually stopped working for us, and it hasn't worked at all the past two weeks. I thought perhaps the computer controlling the mix and reaction was malfunctioning, or there was a variable we hadn't accounted for. But then some very peculiar things started happening in the city."

"What sort of peculiar things?" the Doctor asked.

"Old, standard batteries have stopped working properly," Elizabeth replied. "For instance, the lithium motherboard batteries in our computers either failed or started producing too much current; we had to pull them all to keep our computers from frying. The lab's power is supplied by our own hydrogen fuel cell, of course, since the city plant is unreliable at best. But after the battery incident we added a new power supply monitor, and it had to filter out some truly strange power fluctuations from our cell. I did some checking, and it seems that every few days—right around dawn—there's a tremendous power drain all over the city. And it's getting worse. At least here we have backup power sources, but I find it quite worrisome, thinking of all those people out there with pacemakers and mechanical hearts whose batteries might randomly fail."

The Doctor nodded. "Quite so, quite so. And I'm sure you've considered the biological implications of this electrical instability trend progressing?"

Elizabeth looked pained. "Honestly, that's a hard thing to even think about."

"What biological implications?" Ace asked.

"Our bodies run on electricity," the Doctor replied. "The nerve signals that let us move, let us breathe, let us think, let our hearts keep beating—it's all electrical."

"Oh. Right," said Ace. "That's a problem then, innit?"

"It's gone way beyond electricity," said Elizabeth. "Yesterday...well, my assistant can explain it best, I think." She turned toward a nearby computer station. "Viktor, please come here and tell these people what happened to you."

A young dark-haired man of about 23 stood up and nervously approached the trio.

"Please take apologies," Viktor said. "My English, not so good. Always thought mathematics enough to talk science."

The young man cleared his throat, looking embarrassed. "I swear to you, I do not drink or stay awake too long yesterday...but walking home near Technical University, I see dragon flying through sky with queen riding it like horse."

"A dragon—as in fire-breathing? With a queen riding on its back?" Ace asked.

Viktor nodded. "Very beautiful, both of them. Dragon very fierce-looking, but not breathing fire that I could see. Queen wearing regal-looking gown and jeweled crown. Should not be on Zikova Street, for sure."

"Thank you, Viktor," Elizabeth said.

After Viktor had gone back to his station, Elizabeth pulled the Doctor and Ace aside. "Viktor isn't the only one here who's reported seeing such...*odd* things. In fact, I daresay that every person you see here has reported a similar sighting—not of the dragon and the queen, but other strange creatures."

"Such as?" asked the Doctor.

"Dancing devils, Griffins, a bear, eagle, and fish strolling through the streets."

The Doctor furrowed his brow. "How on *earth* does a fish stroll?"

"On its fins," replied Elizabeth. "But there are two characteristics that all the sightings have in common, Doctor. First, it's only the night-time sightings that coincide with the power outages—there's almost no trouble with batteries and generators or the power plant during the daytime hours."

"No exceptions there?"

"Yes—on those days when there is rain or heavy cloud cover, the power outages are rampant. But here's the other thing, Doctor: all of my assistants have reported that these creatures, these...*apparitions*, whatever you want to call them, all of them look as if they were, well..."

"Out with it, Elizabeth," said the Doctor. "Your grandmother was never one to mince words; I assume that you have inherited her gift for straightforwardness, as well."

Elizabeth took a deep breath, released it, and said: "Everyone says that the beings—although solidly three-dimensional—look as if they were drawn by an artist in pen and ink, or perhaps charcoal."

The Doctor straightened. "*Really*? How absolutely fascinating. Tell me, have any of your assistants reported any physical evidence that may support their sightings?"

Elizabeth nodded. "Viktor says that the dragon's wings smashed in a large section of the Hostel *Dejvice's* entrance and first few floors. Thank goodness the hostel is empty, being temporarily closed for business due to the energy shortage."

"Indeed," muttered the Doctor, tapping the handle of his umbrella. "Are there any more particulars that we need to know? Leave out no detail, regardless of how tiny, insignificant, or rather silly it may seem."

Elizabeth grinned. "I *knew* Grandmother was right about you!" She turned to face the lab and clapped her hands as she announced: "Everyone—your attention, please. I'm calling an emergency meeting in the lower lounge, *right now*. Viktor, since you've already spoken with the Doctor, you may remain here to monitor the machines. Everyone else, please go downstairs now."

The Doctor leaned over toward Ace and whispered, "I do so admire a woman who knows how to take charge."

"Oh, right!" protested Ace. "You're all full of respect for the take-charge type of woman, unless of course it's *me* ordering you about."

"This isn't the time to argue pedantics, Ace, come. Time and tide melt the snowman and all that."

"It's 'Time and tide wait for'—oh, never mind!"

They followed Elizabeth and the others downstairs to the lounge.

"Any other time, any other place," said Ace to the Doctor as she stared up at the slightly overcast sky above the church, "and I'd swear we'd just spent the better part of an hour in the loony bin."

"The entirety of the multiverse is a loony bin, dear Ace," replied the Doctor. "One only need know how to speak the language."

Ace laughed. "Well, then, I couldn't ask to be paired up with a better interpreter, could I?"

"I choose to take that as a compliment. If it was meant otherwise, please don't tell me. I'm quite sensitive."

"Here you are," said Elizabeth, joining them on the steps outside the church. "I've marked all the areas where there have been reported sightings over the past several weeks." She offered the rolled-up map to the Doctor, who waved it away.

"No need for that," he said. "I've been here numerous times and know the city quite well, thank you."

"Are you sure?" asked Elizabeth.

"Absolutely," he replied. "The map of Prague is right up here." He tapped his head. "In the old toboggan."

"Well, *you* may know the layout of the city," said Ace, taking the map from Elizabeth, "but I'm still a first-time tourist. Thank you, Elizabeth. I'm sure this will prove useful, should the Doctor and I be separated."

"Your confidence in my powers of navigation is deeply touching," said the Doctor.

Elizabeth grinned at the both of them, and then added: "The eye-witness accounts suggest that most of the activity has been seen heading to or from an area near the Jewish Quarter. Something tells me that the source of the problem may be centered there."

The Doctor slapped his hands together. "Very well, then—near the Jewish Quarter it shall be. Perhaps we'll catch a glimpse of good Rabbi Loew's Golem, eh? Wouldn't that be exciting?"

Ace shrugged. "Says you."

The Doctor turned toward Elizabeth. "One last thing—I listened very carefully to your assistants' accounts, and I don't recall hearing *one* of them mention anything about the phenomena coming from or returning to an area 'near the Jewish Quarter.'" He stared at her unblinking. "What did *you* see, Elizabeth?"

"How did you know?"

"Elementary, my dear Holub. Every person in your lab reported at least *two* encounters with the phenomena, while you, evidently, have spent the whole of your life secluded in this gargantuan edifice, never seeing so much as a bird building its nest. As oddities, go, I'd call that one of the more intriguing ones—wouldn't you agree, Ace?"

"*Does* seem a bit off, now that you mention it."

The Doctor tapped the tip of his umbrella against the stone stairs. "Right! So, I ask once again—what did *you* see, Elizabeth?"

Elizabeth looked down at her feet, sighed, then faced the Doctor. "Understand, Doctor, that my position here requires that my staff has the utmost, unshakable confidence in my leadership abilities, and—"

"—and you don't wish to sound daft, lest you lose that confidence. Yes, yes, I understand your reasons for keeping your personal encounters to yourself, but you needn't worry about Ace and mw thinking you incontinent."

"'Incompetent'," Ace corrected.

"Right you are. So, Elizabeth?"

"I was in the Little Quarter, visiting the new branch of the National Library, and decided to pay a visit to Prague Castle—it's just over the Charles Bridge, on the other side of the Jewish Quarter."

Unable to maintain eye contact with the Doctor—whose glare was becoming intensely impatient—Elizabeth addressed Ace. "I fancy myself something of an architecture buff, and Prague has some of the most beautiful buildings in the world—none more so than Prague Castle."

"Travelogues bore me to tears, Elizabeth," said the Doctor.

"And she ain't talking to *you*, now, is she?" snapped Ace.

The Doctor pouted. "No reason to be cross about it. I have feelings too, you know."

"The thing is," Elizabeth continued, "a section of the castle was destroyed in the petrol riots—a bomb brought down an entire tower. But that tower, just the other night...*it was back*."

"You mean it, like, reappeared while you were watching?"

"No," replied Elizabeth. "I mean it was still there, as if it had never been destroyed. Not a stone out of place. And I heard...I heard *music* from somewhere inside, a—"

"—a violin?" asked Ace.

"Yes! How did you know?"

The Doctor turned toward his companion. "Indeed, I should like to know the answer to that myself."

"Not important," said Ace, sliding the map into a side pocket of her rucksack. "We need to get moving. If the electricity goes out at nightfall, we've got about six hours."

"I assume, Elizabeth," said the Doctor, "that you will be willing to lend us your car."

"But you need to know what I saw!" said Elizabeth.

"Yes...?" said the Doctor.

"A giant. A great, fierce-looking thing."

"A giant?" said Ace. "As in 'fee-fi-fo-fum'?"

Elizabeth nodded. "Precisely."

"Oh, this just gets better 'n better, don't it, Professor?"

"And on my way back across the bridge," continued Elizabeth, "I saw a knight conversing with a large earthworm."

Ace caught the glint in the Doctor's eyes: a sparkle of almost-realization that told her in no uncertain terms he was already piecing things together. Despite his sometimes exasperating her, it was at moments like this, when she could almost hear his mind going *clickety-clickety-click!*, that she found him unquestionably compelling—even attractive, in his own peculiar way.

Elizabeth escorted them to her subcompact hydrogen car and gave the keys to Ace. "I'm assuming that the good Doctor's driving skills have not improved with age," she said.

The Doctor sighed. "Everyone's insulting me today."

Ace pointed toward the car. "Get in, Professor."

"I live to serve."

And with that, Elizabeth wished them luck, and Ace and the Doctor climbed inside.

Ace was just starting the car when the Doctor reached over and took firm hold of her arm.

"Out with it, Ace."

"With what?"

"How did you know about the violin music?"

"Does it matter?"

The Doctor glared at her. "Listen carefully to me, Ace. The tower Elizabeth spoke of is called Dalibor Tower. It was built as part of the fortifications to Prague Castle by King Vladislav Jagiello.

"The tower also served as a prison. It was given its name after its first inmate, Dalibor of Kozojedy, a knight sentenced to death for supporting a peasant rebellion. He was placed in a pit, an underground dungeon. He played the violin to pass the time and prevent himself from going mad from the isolation. People came to listen to him play. I know this because the story was used by Bedrich Smetana in his opera *Dalibor*—the debut of which I was fortunate enough to attend in this very city. So I must ask you a very important question, Ace—*how did you know*?"

"I heard it in a dream."

"The dream you spoke of back in the TARDIS?"

"Yes."

"And I take it, then, that you also saw the dungeon-pit?"

"Yes. There was a little girl kneeling over it. She was talking to her father—her father was the one down in the pit, the one playing the violin."

The Doctor shook his head. "Impossible. Dalibor of Kozojedy never sired any children."

"Maybe it weren't Dalibor she was talking to."

"Then who *would* she have been–?" The Doctor waved his hand. "Never mind, the identity of the violinist isn't our immediate problem. That little girl and Dalibor Tower is. I assume, dear Ace, that you would recognize this little girl should we cross paths with her?"

She nodded. "I'd know that face anywhere. She was laughing in my dream, but there was...there was a sadness about her, a sort of loneliness. I knew just how she was feeling."

The Doctor gave her hand a tender, affectionate squeeze. "You're not alone anymore, Ace. Never will be, if I've anything to say about it. Now, I suggest you start the vehicle and drive in the direction of Charles Bridge."

Ace reached for the map, and then realized that she *had* said a few things today that might have hurt the Doctor's feelings, and the Doctor did need to know that her trust in him was unshaken. "Which way?"

The Doctor smiled at her, and then pointed. "That-a-way, Pardner—as John Wayne used to say."

They had been traveling for less than an hour when they spotted the first dragon, this one queen-less but rather imposing, nonetheless. It was stretched out by the roadside soaking up the sunlight. The creature—though fully three-dimensional—appeared to have been drawn, in the greatest detail, with charcoal: its uniform grayness stood in stark contrast to the lush field of green on which it lay.

"Pull over," said the Doctor.

"Stop beside a dragon? Are you daft?"

"Always. Now pull over. I have a hunch."

"And you wonder why I worry." Ace pulled over, and the Doctor immediately climbed out but did not approach the Dragon. Since the Doctor's attention was elsewhere, Ace took the opportunity to reach behind her and dig a canister of Nitro-9—one of six she'd secretly brought along—from her rucksack. She placed it down by her right side where the Doctor couldn't see and curled her finger around the activation pin.

"Hello?" called the Doctor. "Hello, my good fellow!"

The dragon opened one sleepy eye, stretched, wiggled, then said: "Are you Hynek? Come in search of the three doves?"

"Hynek?" replied the Doctor. "I'm afraid not. I'm known as the Doctor. I hate to bother you, seeing as how you're obviously having a grand old time sunbathing, but I was wondering if you might know the quickest route to Prague Castle. My companion and I are in a bit of hurry, so any—"

The Doctor's words cut off, and after a moment Ace leaned over toward his side of the vehicle. "Professor? You all right?"

The Doctor leaned down. "Did he say 'Hynek'?"

"That's how it sounded to me."

"Ah." He stood up again and continued his conversation with the dragon. "If you'd be so kind to point us in the right direction..."

The dragon raised up its left wing and flicked it southward.

Tipping his hat, the Doctor said, "I thank you for your kindness, good Sir Dragon."

"You haven't by chance a sheep you could spare, have you?" asked the dragon. "I could fancy a snack right about now."

"So sorry, fresh out of sheep, I'm afraid. I might be able to locate a chocolate bar, though."

"No, thank you," said the dragon. "Chocolate doesn't very much agree with me. Ah, well...." And the dragon closed its eyes, stretched out in the sunlight, and fell back asleep, though not before mumbling something about three doves and dancing devils.

The Doctor leapt back into the car, slamming closed the door and hissing, "We must make haste, Ace, to the nearest library or bookstore. The first one we pass, stop. *The very first one.*"

Ace pulled away with a bit more speed than was called for; if the Doctor noticed, he said nothing.

"What's going on, Professor? Why do we need to go shopping for a *book*?"

"Not just any book, oh, no—it's a very specific book I've in mind. And it *must* be the correct edition!"

"Got a sudden urge to read, have you?"

"A sudden *need*, dear Ace." He turned toward her. "If my hunch is correct, then we may very well be dealing with something infinitely more threatening than the loss of the city's power and the presence of these fantastical beings."

"And what would that be?"

The Doctor opened his mouth to speak, closed it, tapped the handle of his umbrella, and then said, "Not just yet. I have to make certain that my hunch is correct."

"That's not fair! I'm entitled to know what we're going up against!"

The Doctor stared at her. "Tell me, Ace, when you spent all that time alone when you were a child, did you ever find solace in fairy stories?"

Ace pulled in a deep breath; the Doctor's question had opened doors in her memory that she'd prefer remained closed forever. "I don't want to talk about it."

The Doctor once again squeezed her hand. "You've given me my answer. We need never speak of this again, unless of course you feel compelled to share with me."

By the time Ace managed to navigate the roads and side-streets leading to the Little Quarter, the sky was growing dim as more clouds crowded the horizon. Though enough sunlight managed to break through to give her a clear field of vision, the shadows were massing for a final attack.

"Not much daylight left, it looks like," she commented.

"Oh, going by the clock, there's still well over three hours of daylight remaining," said the Doctor as he leaned forward and looked up through the windshield. "However, I'd say that the elements are conspiring against us. If you'll look around us, Ace, you'll see that there are fewer cars on the road and more horse-drawn wagons. It would appear the citizens of Prague are as resourceful as ever. They *know* the electricity is going to fail them as soon as the lights fades, and they've found a way to adapt—at least, as far as their transportation needs go."

"Tell that to the bloke with the tricky pacemaker in his chest. I'm sure he'll find a lot of comfort in that."

"Point taken. The branch of the National Library should be just round this bend."

As indeed it was; a towering, elegant, Gothic-style stone building with numerous Baroque additions, the place looked to Ace more like a cathedral than a place to house books—but of course, as the Doctor would undoubtedly point out to her, all libraries *were* a sort of cathedral, when you thought about it.

"Impressive," said the Doctor; then, to Ace: "Or if I may borrow your term of choice, '*Wicked*'."

"No arguments here," replied Ace. She was just pulling into a parking space when the car completely stopped; the engine died, the dashboard lights cut out, and the radio—which Ace had been playing at a low volume—snapped off.

"Well, well," said the Doctor. "It appears that the clouds have at last ruled the day—or what remains of it."

Ace looked out her window. All around the Quarter, lights were going out; no sooner did the electricity in one building cease to function than someone inside began lighting numerous candles. Even the interior of the library began to sparkle with dozens of small dancing flames.

"Now what?" she asked.

Opening his door, the Doctor replied, "We go in search of the needed book. Come, Ace, we must basin."

"'Hasten.'"

"Have it your way."

They scurried up the stone stairs leading to the magnificent wooden doors of the entrance, but no sooner had they reached the landing than the Doctor was knocked backward by some invisible force, losing his balance and dropping firmly on his backside, his Panama hat falling from his head.

But his was not the only hat Ace saw on the landing; as soon as the Doctor collided with whatever invisible barrier had stopped him, a well-worn cap fell to the landing, as well, seemingly from thin air.

At the same instant the cap became visible, a young-ish lad dressed in woolen peasant rags and carrying an ancient rucksack appeared; no more than seventeen, looking several centuries out of date in dress and manner, he, too, had been knocked on his backside.

"Hello," said Ace, looking back and forth between the two. "What's this, then?"

"*This*," said the doctor, getting back on his feet and snatching up not only his hat but the stranger's cap, as well, "is one Sleepy John, unless I am mistaken."

Sleepy John looked wide-eyed at the Doctor as he rose to his feet. "I'm afraid you have me at a great disadvantage, sir. You know my name, but I don't recall our ever having met before."

"I'm known as the Doctor, and we *have* met before, my good fellow—many times, in fact. I know your tale well. Have you located the secret place where the Queen is off to every night? I imagine the King is exasperated with concern."

"Hold on," said Ace. "I don't mean to seem rude, but I think I'm entitled to know—"

The Doctor faced her. "We no longer need to go inside the library, dear Ace. Bumping into Sleepy John here has now told me all we need to know." And with that, he removed his Panama hat, slipped on Sleepy John's cap, and immediately disappeared.

"Professor?" yelled Ace, suddenly feeling panic. "Professor, where–?"

"Right where I was," came the Doctor's voice. A moment later, he removed the cap; both he and it were quite visible again. "An odd feeling, invisibility. Really, Sleepy John, I don't know how you put up with it. That…queasy feeling in one's stomach."

"After a while, you no longer notice or mind," replied John. "No discomfort is too much to endure for the sake of my mistress's content."

The Doctor shot a quick *aha*! glance at Ace. "Your mistress, you say?"

"I do."

Ace, now frustrated and more than a bit anxious, yanked the Doctor's hat from his head and took John's cap, as well. "All right, then! Neither one of you are going to get your stupid hats back until one of you tells me, right now, what's going on!"

The Doctor pointed at Ace but addressed John. "She's got a lot of spirit."

"'Tis an odd name for a lady so delicate and lovely," said John.

"*Odd*?" shouted Ace. "What's so odd about—hello. Did you just call me 'delicate and lovely'?"

"Aye," replied John, bowing gracefully, taking hold of her hand, and kissing it.

Ace slowly pulled back her had, red-faced, and desperately trying not to giggle.

"The fellow you are looking at, my delicate and lovely Ace," said the Doctor, "is none other than Sleepy John, a character from a book published in 1917 by Unwin Brothers Limited, the Gresham Press, Woking and London. The book in question is called *Czech Folk Tales*, the stories in its table of contents having been selected and translated by Dr. Josef Baudis, M.R.I.A., Lecturer in Comparative Philology at the Prague University.

"If the appearance of the dragon we saw back on the road—as well as those beings described by Elizabeth's assistants—struck you as odd, it's because they are three-dimensional recreations of the illustrations contained in that very book, drawn by...let me see now—ah, yes, I have it! The first two illustrations are copies of pictures by Joseph Manes; the others were drawn by E. Stan k, who in some case has adopted drawings by Mikuláš Aleš."

"I don't believe it," said Ace, gawking at Sleepy John.

"Believe it," replied the Doctor.

"May I ask, Doctor," said John, "if you, too, seek not only the Queen but the princess and the three roses?"

"What did you say? The princess?"

John gave a nod of his head. "And the three roses."

The Doctor folded his arms across his chest, then raised one hand to scratch at his forehead. "This is very strange, very strange, indeed."

Ace looked at him. "Stranger than bumping into monsters and characters from an old storybook?"

"I should say so, yes. Give me a moment to think." He turned away from them, facing the street.

"M'lady," whispered John to Ace. "I don't wish to appear discourteous, but will you give back my cap so I can be on my way?" He turned slightly so that Ace could see the contents of his rucksack; vegetables, fruits, fresh meats and poultry, a small cask of water, and several boxes of matches. "My mistress has not eaten in three days, and I must get this food to her."

"Did you steal this food from the marketplace? While wearing this?" She held up his cap.

"Aye, that I did."

Ace thought that—if one were forced into a situation where food must be stolen in order to survive—it was dashed clever to enlist someone who could make himself invisible.

"I think," she said to John, "that your mistress is someone we need to talk to."

"My mistress talks to no one but we who live to serve her. She has no desire to be part of the affairs of man or his implements of power."

"'Implements of power'? What you mean by that?"

John pointed to a darkened street light, the unmoving cars in the street, even the phone lines on their towers. "My mistress lost her father to the great battle over such power many years ago. He was...he was killed in a most brutal fashion."

"*The petrol riots,*" said Ace, more to herself than to John. "Was her...was your mistress's father, was he killed when Dalibor Tower was destroyed?"

"Aye, and a great conflagration it was. He had hidden her elsewhere in the castle where she would be safe from harm, but he himself fell victim to the brutality of the mobs." John looked at his feet. "He was crushed when the tower came down. He lived for nearly two days afterward, trapped beneath the rubble. My mistress knelt beside the ruins talking to him, trying to keep him alive. But it was all for naught. His death broke her young heart. She took the only possession she had remaining—the book of which the Doctor spoke, a gift from her father—and retreated into the castle, never to venture out into the evil world of men and their power again."

"The batteries, the electricity, the generators, all of it," said Ace to herself. "She's drawing on that power to bring you to life! *That's why the sightings continue after the sun goes down*!"

"And why the entire city experiences massive power surges at dawn every few days," said the Doctor, rejoining the two of them. "The girl must sleep sometime, and no doubt her waking causes a moment or two of tremendous confusion and disorientation, thus the surges. Excellent deduction, Ace. During the day, this girl draws her power from the sun—it's child's play to convert solar energy into electricity—but at night...ah, at night she has no choice but to draw her power from every available source of man-made energy. And seeing how she hates it so—after all, the fight for energy cost her father's life—she would have no regrets whatsoever about doing so. Electricity, batteries, generators, all of it, is evil in her eyes. It's what killed her father."

John once again nodded his head. "Aye, good Doctor. She has spoken of her hatred for it often."

"As she understandably would. But what puzzles me—well, there are several things that puzzle me at the moment, so why don't we address them in order?

"One: the last petrol riot in Prague was over fifteen years ago. May I ask, Sleepy John, how old is your mistress?"

"Eight-hundred-twenty-five days and a thousand."

The Doctor's eyes grew wide. "*Five years old*? Oh, dear me, Ace, this is worse than I feared."

"How d'ya mean?"

"Remember when I told you that we may very well be up against something infinitely more dangerous than a simple series of power outages and these sightings of strange creatures?"

"Yes."

He put a hand on her shoulder. "Well, my dear companion, we are facing what is perhaps the most dangerous opponent we've yet encountered—the iron will of a child's imagination, a child who also has the power to make her fantasies sentient in order to act against a world she hates. If she's been secluded for this long, then of course she'd have no idea of the medical technologies people rely upon—pacemakers and such—and so would have no idea the harm she's causing, the danger she's inflicting on the people of this city."

Ace stared at him. "I'm not sure she'd care if she *did* know, Professor. If the petrol riot that killed her father was fifteen years ago, then she ought to be—"

"—there is no room in her universe for what *ought* to be, Ace. She retreated into Prague castle and, in essence, froze time for her and those who, like Sleepy John, exist only in her imagination."

Ace felt her throat tighten and her eyes begin to tear. "Oh, that poor little thing. How...how *lonely* she must be!"

"Quite so," said the Doctor. Then, to John: "Where was I?"

"You were about to ask your second question."

"Ah, yes, thank you. Two: You say that you are also in search of a princess and three roses, correct?"

"Aye."

"Fascinating. Three: why were you here at the library?"

"My mistress sent me to retrieve the very book of which you spoke—and to fetch the two of you, should I have the opportunity to find you."

"Why did she want the book?"

"I think it not a matter of her wanting it, good Doctor. I think it a matter of her wanting you *not* to have it. I must confess that it puzzled me, as she already has a copy."

"Yes, a last gift from her father, I heard. So your mistress has been aware of our presence in this city since we arrived, I take it?"

"Aye."

The Doctor looked at Ace. "Good Lord, what tremendous, incredible, *startling* power she must possess." Then, to Sleepy John: "My good sir, would you be so kind as to escort us to your mistress?"

"I have a wagon with horses waiting across the road."

Both Ace and the Doctor looked to where John was pointing.

"I don't see anything," said Ace.

"That's because the same enchantment that enables Sleepy John to become invisible has been extended to anything his mistress deems necessary—isn't that right, John?"

"Aye."

"Well, I daresay, Ace, that you and I are about to attract some curious stares, as we'll be floating along in the air."

"No, good Doctor," said John, producing two more caps from his sack. "I've been instructed to ask you to wear these so that none will see us and be tempted to follow."

Taking his cap from Ace—but not yet placing it on his head—John began to descend the stairs, gesturing for Ace and the Doctor to follow.

"I hope you brought the sonic screwdriver with you, Professor."

"It would do us no good, Ace. Its power source is man-made." He took hold of her arm. "Besides, should the need arise—and I do so hope it does not—we have those canisters of Nitro-9 that you think I don't know you smuggled out of the TARDIS."

"No one's ever known me as well as you, Professor." Ace reached down and took hold of his hand. "Or accepted me as you have."

"Yes, well...I don't know who else but you would put up with the likes of me, so we're well-paired, don't you think?"

"I do."

They smiled at one another as they followed Sleepy John down the stairs and across the street.

"What else is puzzling you?" asked Ace. "Don't try to deny it, Professor—you've got that 'I-still-don't-know-all-the-answers' look about you."

"Perceptiveness is your middle name. The dragon by the road earlier, he asked about three doves and spoke of dancing devils, did he not?"

"Yes."

"And Sleepy John, he says his quest is not only to discover where the Queen goes at night, but to find the princess and the three roses."

Ace shrugged. "Seems simple enough to me."

The Doctor stopped and turned to face her, taking hold of her shoulders. "But it's *not* simple, dear Ace, not simple at all! We have encountered two characters from the book, yet they have told us that they are involved in some way with elements from...let me see...at least *six* different stories! Sleepy John had nothing to do with the princess or the three roses—those are two completely separate tales from his. The dancing devils of which the dragon spoke? *Those* are from Sleepy John's story."

"It's all mixed up then, innit?"

"Very much so, I'm afraid. Which can mean only one of two things, dear Ace: either the girl's storybook has fallen apart and she has misassembled the pages, thus confusing the story elements, or..."

"...or she's gone out of her mind from the hatred and loneliness."

"Not unlike those prisoners kept in the pit of Dalibor Tower. I rather prefer my theory to yours."

"Me, too."

"Well, we'll know soon enough," said the Doctor, looking out into the growing darkness.

"Would you be cross with me if I told you I was scared?" asked Ace.

"Not if you won't be cross with me for sharing your sentiment—squared."

They joined Sleepy John in the invisible wagon—after much fumbling about on both their parts—then donned their caps and vanished from the sight of man.

All of the storybooks characters were lining the road as they climbed from the wagon and followed Sleepy John into the tower; princesses, griffins, dancing devils, numerous dragons, hairy beasties, even the bear, eagle, and strolling fish were there. Ace was overwhelmed at the amount of people and creatures that bade them welcome, and as she studied them she saw the great detail that had gone into their drawing, and was once again amazed that any human being could possess the gift to create something so lifelike, so utterly *real*, from the ether of their imagination. She thought of how, as a child, she had wished for such a talent, something to make her popular with the other children, but she'd been an orphan, an outcast, with only her fists and her quick temper to protect her from the others' cruelty.

Even though she'd not yet seen this little girl, she felt that she knew Sleepy John's mistress as well as she knew herself; angry, confused, sad, and so very, very alone and lonely.

The thought nearly tore her in half, and made her feel even more grateful for the time storm that had whisked her away and dropped her in the Doctor's path. She'd not known a truly lonely moment since meeting him...nor a dull one, for that matter.

They followed John into the tower and up a seemingly unending winding staircase until they at last reached a wide, deep, dark chamber that was so chilly Ace could actually see her breath. In the distance a small fire burned, the flames contained by a circle of stones to hold the coals in place. beside the fire sat the little girl from her dream, staring down languorously into a pit in the floor.

Ace felt the Doctor's hand on her arm.

"We must proceed with the greatest caution, dear Ace."

"I know." She could not move her stare from the little girl's face; so pale, so drawn, with circles under the eyes far too dark for a child so young. Despite her better and more intelligent instincts, Ace wanted nothing so much at that moment than to run over and hold the little girl in her arms and whisper, "*It's all right, love, it's all right, I'll be your friend, I'll make it all better.*"

"Please wait here," said Sleepy John, "whilst I speak with my mistress."

"Of course," said the Doctor.

With a bow, John was off.

"She's so *small,*" said Ace. "She looks more like a girl of three than five."

"I imagine that living in these conditions for so long has not been of the greatest benefit to her physiology."

Ace glared at him. "*Must* you talk about it in such clinical terms?"

"If I am to keep my nerves intact, dear Ace, then, yes, I must."

"What's the matter with your nerves?"

The Doctor slowly raised the tip of his umbrella and pointed toward a distant corner where a massive shadow dislodged itself from the darkness and moved toward the firelight.

The giant ogre's face was a twisted mass of scars and infantile rage. Its mighty arms bulged with muscle and sinew, and in each of its enormous hands it held a large block of stone.

Its stare was intensely focused on the Doctor and Ace.

"Her bodyguard, I would imagine," whispered the Doctor. "And from the looks of him, we could not possibly outrun those stones should he decide to chuck them in our direction. I suggest we remain quite still for the moment."

The ogre snarled quietly, and as if to confirm the Doctor's suspicions, lifted the stones and nodded toward the two of them.

"I'll bet he's got wicked aim," whispered Ace.

"That goes without saying."

Ace slowly slipped her hand into a pocket of her rucksack and grasped a Nitro-9 canister.

"No," said the Doctor, grasping her arm tighter. "Despite the considerable size of this room, it is still an enclosed space. We might harm the girl—not to mention bring the tower down around us."

Ace released her grip on the canister, but left her hand resting against it, nonetheless; it made her feel safe.

Sleepy John finished speaking with the little girl, then rose and turned toward the Doctor and Ace. "My mistress requests the pleasure of your company."

Slowly, the Doctor and Ace walked toward her; as they did so, the ogre moved closer until it towered behind them, holding the great stones over their heads.

"This is most distressing," whispered the Doctor.

"Hush," said Ace.

"Hello," said the little girl. "My name is Nápev."

"'Melody'," said the Doctor. "Your name is Czechoslovakian for 'Melody'."

"*Melody*," said Ace. "What a lovely name—what a *beautiful* name."

"Thank you," said Nápev. "Papa chose it. He always said I was like a song."

Ace smiled. "How wonderful."

"Mama died when I was born. Papa and I, we lived here until the bad people came."

"I know," said Ace. "We—the Doctor and I—we know all about how terrible things have been for you, and we came to help."

Nápev studied her face for a moment, and then said, "You're not going to try and take Papa and all my friends away, are you?"

"No, of course not."

"Ace," said the Doctor. "Be careful what you promise her."

"I don't think I like him," said Nápev. "He reminds me of the people who took Papa away."

Ace looked at the Doctor and dismissed him with a wave of her hand. "Oh, don't be bothered by him—he has a strange way about him, and he can be a royal pain, but he's very smart, and very kind."

"Really?"

"Cross my heart."

Nápev looked at the Doctor. "Should I smash him? You could stay here with me. We could be friends. Papa would play such wonderful music for us."

"No!" shouted Ace. "No, please, don't...don't hurt him. You see, he's my best friend, my *only* friend, really—unless you want to be my friend."

Nápev reached out with a trembling hand and touched Ace's cheek. "You're not like the others," she said. "Sleepy John and the rest." She knelt down and rummaged through a pile of rubbish, at last finding what she was looking for—a book; a very tattered, damaged book, with a broken spine and loose pages stuffed back inside in the wrong order. "Papa read to me from this, such wonderful stories—and he could read them so *well*."

"Oh, I've no doubt about that," said Ace, taking the book from Nápev and showing it to the Doctor. "I'm sorry that it's fallen apart on you like this."

"That's all right," said Nápev, taking the book from Ace and holding it against her chest like most little girls would hold a favorite doll. "I remember how he read them, and I remember the stories. Did your papa ever read stories to you?"

Ace shook her head. "No. I don't have a father, or a mum, really. I was...I was left on my own when I was very young."

"I'm sorry," said Nápev.

Ace reached out and took the little girl's hand. "It's a terrible thing, innit? To be alone, to have no one to play with or talk to except for people and things you make up or read about."

"Did they laugh at you?" asked Nápev. "Did they shout cruel words at you and throw things and chase you into dark places?"

Ace felt a tear slip from her eye and slide down her face. "Yes, they did. I was completely alone until I met the Doctor."

"What's your name?"

"Everybody calls me 'Ace", but you can call me by my real name: Dorothy."

"Good heavens," said the Doctor from behind them. "This is quite the honor being bestowed upon you, Nápev. Were I ever to call her 'Dorothy', she would most certainly 'clean my clock', as goes the saying."

"He talks funny," said Nápev.

"You'll get used to it."

"Why are you crying?" asked Nápev. "Did the man in the funny hat hurt you?" She glared at the Doctor. "I can still smash him, if you want."

"No, please, that won't be necessary—but I'll keep that in mind." She cast a quick glance over her shoulder at the Doctor, and then winked at him.

But Nápev was nothing if not persistent. "So why are you crying?"

"*Because*," Ace replied, "I see how cold and dark it is in here, and I remember what it was like when I lived on the streets of London. To grow up motherless, fatherless, friendless...to never dance with a boy, never have someone who loves you there to tuck you in at night, someone you know will still be there for you in the morning...to have no one to depend on, or who depends on you, who *loves* you...it hardens your heart too soon, and the world will do that soon enough."

She reached out and gently pulled Nápev toward her. "You've not had a childhood, and that is truly cruel, and you so deserve to be happy, Melody. You *do*! Please, *please* let the Doctor and me help you."

Nápev laid her head against Ace's shoulder. "How can you help me?"

"I know a place," said the Doctor. "I know a place where you will have many people, many friends who will care for you, who will teach you how to use your abilities without—well, without harming others."

Nápev's head snapped up. "I've never *hurt anyone*! *They* hurt Papa! They killed him!"

"I am aware of that," said the Doctor. "But you must understand, Nápev, that those people who did this terrible thing to you and your father, they're long since dead or in prison and cannot harm you any longer. But when you summon forth your friends like Sleepy John and the dragons and this rather unnerving fellow who's holding these stones over my head, you...how to put this?"

"It hurts people," Ace said. "I know you don't mean for it to, but it does."

"But all I do is drink in the magic. It's all around. I feel it in the air, in my head, on my skin, all the time."

Ace looked at the Doctor with pleading in her glistening eyes.

"That magic, Nápev," he said, "is what helps the people of this city to live. It's what helps them care for their children, their pets, their friends. When you drink the magic so as to bring forth your friends, the people who live outside the walls of this castle, they cannot take care of their children. They cannot tuck them into warm beds because it's so cold. They cannot make food for their breakfast." He leaned forward. "They cannot read stories to them as your father did to you because they have no light by which to see their books."

Nápev's eyes began tearing. "I didn't know."

"Well, now you do. Will you be a good little girl and stop drinking the magic?"

"But all of my friends will go away. Papa will leave me."

"Oh, no, dear child, that won't happen at all." The Doctor knelt beside Nápev and Ace, placing a finger against the child's forehead. "They will stay with you in here." Then he touched her chest above her heart. "And here. And when we take you to this place I know of, you can call them out as often as wish and it will hurt no one. Your father can play his violin as much as he wants, and the dragons can fly, and the fish can stroll, and Sleepy John can still run to market and fetch food for you. Nothing will change—except, of course, for your surroundings."

"Is it a nice place?"

"Yes, it is. Particularly for a child of your talent."

Ace glared at him. "You're talking about *Gallifrey*, aren't you?"

"Yes. Nápev will find herself and her friends most welcome there."

"How do you know they'll—?"

"I still have friends, Ace. Some of them on the Council. Gallifrey will be the best place for our Nápev, I promise."

"Is it far?" asked Nápev.

"Oh, very," replied the Doctor. "Across the expanse of the universe. Oh, the adventure we'll have while traveling there! Have you ever seen the stars so close that you could reach out and touch them, Nápev? Have you ever flown through space on the wings of time? Have you ever seen a supernova?"

Wide-eyed, Nápev shook her head. “It sounds so *beautiful.*”

“Well, imagine how much more thrilling the trip will be with your father there to play music for all of us, eh?” The Doctor offered his hand. “If you’ll release the magic back to the people of this city, we’ve only to walk back to where our spaceship awaits, and then—*zoom*, we’re off to the stars with the entire cosmos our playground.”

In a blink—a literal blink of Ace’s eyes—the ogre and Sleepy John vanished. Ace had no choice but to assume that the other beings outside were gone, as well.

From a small opening high up on the farthest wall, the glow of streetlights flowed inside.

“Thank you, Nápev,” said the Doctor, helping the child to her feet and leading her toward the stairway. “You’ll have a most glorious time on our trip, I promise you.”

Ace caught up with them, and though they had to walk single-file down the winding staircase, once outside, Nápev immediately got between Ace and the Doctor. Each of them took hold of one of the little girl’s hands as they walked from the tower and toward the bridge.

“Lovely night, isn’t it?” asked the Doctor, nodding upward at the glowing streetlamps and the sparkling, warm lights from inside the houses they passed.

“Papa and I never had a house like those,” said Nápev.

“You will,” said Ace.

“Promise?”

Ace looked at the Doctor, who gave a quick nod of his head.

“Promise,” said Ace.

Nápev then tugged on the Doctor’s hand. “Do you know any good stories? Please tell us a story while we walk.”

“Oh, the *stories* I can tell! Wouldn’t know where to begin.”

“Lucky us,” said Ace.

“Be nice,” said Nápev. “And just for that, *you* get to tell us a story.”

“Oh, my dear Ace,” said the Doctor, smiling, “something tells me this is the beginning of a beautiful friendship.”

And the three of them walked on into the night, the lights from the city guiding them to safety and warmth and grand adventure.

About the Author

Lucy A. Snyder is the four-time Bram Stoker Award-winning author of the novels *Spellbent, Shotgun Sorceress, Switchblade Goddess,* and the collections *Soft Apocalypses, Shooting Yourself in the Head For Fun and Profit: A Writer's Survival Guide, Orchid Carousals, Sparks and Shadows, Chimeric Machines,* and *Installing Linux on a Dead Badger.* Her writing has been translated into French, Russian, and Japanese editions and has appeared in publications such as *Apex Magazine, Nightmare Magazine, Pseudopod, Strange Horizons, Weird Tales, Steampunk World, In the Court of the Yellow King, Shadows Over Main Street, Qualia Nous, The Library of the Dead,* and *Best Horror of the Year, Vol. 5.*

Lucy was born in South Carolina but grew up in grew up in the cowboys-and-cactus part of Texas. She currently lives in Worthington, Ohio with her husband and occasional co-author Gary A. Braunbeck.

Lucy has a BS in biology and an MA in journalism and is a graduate of the 1995 Clarion Science Fiction & Fantasy Writers' Workshop. She has worked as a computer systems specialist, science writer, biology tutor, researcher, software reviewer, radio news editor, and bassoon instructor. She currently mentors students in Seton Hill University's MFA program in Writing Popular Fiction.

If genres were wall-building nations, Lucy's stories would be forging passports, jumping fences, swimming rivers and dodging bullets. You can learn more about her at www.lucysnyder.com and you can follow her on Twitter at @LucyASnyder.

Publication History

"Spinwebs"—*Not Our Kind,* Alliteration Ink, January 2015.

"The Strange Architecture of the Heart"—*Bless Your Mechanical Heart,* Evil Girlfriend Media, March 2014.

"Approaching Lavender"—*Chiral Mad 2,* Written Backwards, December 2013.

"Dura Mater"—*Qualia Nous,* Written Backwards, August 2014.

"The Still-Life Drama of Passing Cars" (co-written with Gary A. Braunbeck)—*Bedtime Stories To Darken Your Dreams* (edited by Alan Clark and Bruce Holland Rogers), IFD Publishing, May 1999. Reprinted in *The Little Orange Book of Odd Stories,* Wildside Press, 2003. Honorable mention, *Year's Best Fantasy and Horror 13.*

"Through Thy Bounty"—Originally appeared in *The Midnighters' Club* anthology, June 2001. Reprinted in *Sparks and Shadows* in 2007, in Apex Online in 2008, and in *LampLight Vol. 2* in 2014. Honorable mention, *Year's Best Fantasy and Horror 15.*

"Cthylla"—*The Library of the Dead,* Written Backwards, May 2015.

"While The Black Stars Burn"—*Cassilda's Song,* Chaosium, August 2015.

"The Abomination of Fensmere"—*Shadows Over Main Street,* Hazardous Press, January 2015.

"The Girl With The Star-Stained Soul"—*In The Court of the Yellow King,* Celaeno Press, September 2014.

"Jessie Shimmer Goes To Hell"—*Manifesto UF,* Angelic Knights Press, September 2013.

"Fable Fusion" (co-written with Gary A. Braunbeck)—*Doctor Who Short Trips: Destination Prague,* Big Finish Productions Ltd., June 2007.

www.ingramcontent.com/pod-product-compliance
Ingram Content Group UK Ltd.
Pitfield, Milton Keynes, MK11 3LW, UK
UKHW041639190726
13854UKWH00006B/2580

9 781935 738770